SPIRITS

Sheri Sebastian-Gabriel

Haverhill House Publishing

This is a work of fiction. Names, characters, places, and incidents either are a product of the authors' imagination or are used fictitiously. Any resemblance to actual events, locales, or persons, living or dead, is entirely coincidental.

SPIRITS

ISBN-13: 978-1-949140-07-1 Hardcover
ISBN-13: 978-1-949140-08-8 Trade Paperback

Cover illustration & design by Dyer Wilk

Haverhill House Publishing
643 E Broadway
Haverhill MA 01830-2420
www.haverhillhouse.com

SPIRITS

"As prospects diminish, as nightmares swell, some pray for Heaven while we live in Hell."

— *The Disease, Echo & the Bunnymen*

For Matt, who always lifts my spirits, and for G, S, and Z, who have infused my life with love.

ACKNOWLEDGMENTS

Spirits would not be possible without the inspiration and love of so many people. Thanks go to John M. McIlveen, Roberta Colasanti, Christopher Golden, James A. Moore, Tony Tremblay, Bracken MacLeod, Dyer Wilk, Keith Minnion, Elizabeth Massie, doungjai gam bepko, Barry DeJasu, Brian Shoopman, Tori Boone, Debbie Vilardi, the late Dr. Joseph Francavilla, Dr. James Owen, Michael Bishop, Jeffrey Ford, and the City of Cape May. I'd also like to thank my three biggest fans, Gabriel, Sebastian, and Zoë, without whom I'd be a shell of a human. Finally, I send my ceaseless gratitude and immortal love to Matt.

CHAPTER 1

The Miller Lite neon's painful electric blue blurred.

Tori knew it was way past time to head home. If she caught the train back to Montclair now, she might even get up bright and early, make some calls, and try to salvage her career. The vodka and tonic melted into oblivion and droplets puddled on the dingy, wooden bar. She clutched the tumbler in trembling fingers. The condensation trickled down her wrist and disappeared somewhere between the pearls of her bracelet.

She gulped the drink like cough syrup, taking the slivers of ice down with the diluted liquor. It was watery with vague hints of alcohol. It didn't make her feel better, but it made her feel less.

The bartender, a pleasant-faced old man with too much pomade in his stark-white hair, leaned on his elbows and clasped his hands together. His lips maneuvered around a set of yellowing teeth.

Tori blinked a few times, not completely sure she understood the words. The jukebox played some up-tempo hit from about thirty years ago, but she couldn't place it. Her ears hummed.

"... another?"

She stared at his mouth, trying to process the muscles moving up and down and sideways and decipher them into English words. He leaned in close enough for her to smell his fishy breath and shouted, “Can. I. Get. You. Another?”

Her back snapped straight in the stool, and she pushed the home button on her phone. The screen light stabbed at her eyes. She squinted. The numbers fuzzed in and out of her vision. The vertical line of a one appeared, but the others were formless.

Sweat prickled under her nose and a trickle slid from her brow. The phone light dimmed, and she lifted her throbbing eyes to the other bar patrons, faceless, interchangeable forms. Another drink seemed like an excellent idea. Her throat itched, and if she could only dull her senses just a little more, she might forget. It might even be possible to drive home with a steady hand, confident in the knowledge that as she maneuvered down Main, the girl wouldn’t be waiting for her, face smashed into the crosswalk in a nightmare so fresh, it could’ve happened yesterday. Was she drunk enough now to escape back to the sanctuary of her home without slamming her brakes to avoid a kid who’d been dead for more than a year?

By the time she looked back up, the bartender was at the other end of the bar tending to one of those formless others. Someone opened the door, and a bitter wind gusted against her skin. It cooled the sweat. She ran her palm from her forehead to her chin and relished the biting chill.

Stevie’s was not her regular watering hole, but it was close to the office. Its clientele were not the hipsters or yuppies that congregated at the sophisticated bars by the train station for an organic beer or acai berry-infused vodka. These were professional drunks, folks who swayed, day in and day out at the bar, drinking straight whiskey. A dust-encrusted Magnavox with foil-lined rabbit ears blipped a Rangers game, but no one seemed to be watching. The walls were stained yellow from cigarette smoke, and the floors were fieldstone with large cracks between each.

Six hours ago—or eight, she couldn't be sure—after Rollie Vasquez sat her down for a face-to-face to discuss her future with the company, she couldn't stave off the tremble that ran from her left elbow all the way to her fingertips.

The hangnail she'd picked at during the meeting ached and puddled with blood at the edges. She absentmindedly twisted it until it broke free from the skin. The blood smeared against her nail, and she plopped it into her mouth and sucked, not really tasting it.

The jagged bit of nail had been irritating her since the night before when she'd ripped it up in bed, the thought of Rollie bringing down the axe eating away at her insides. Even in reflection, her belly tensed. She'd known what the meeting would be about the minute he'd scheduled it. Flaming ulcer pain seized her in the days leading up to it. Chugging down whiskey neat at the Carriage House blurred her head enough that the stomach pain was nothing more than a gurgle of indigestion.

All the extra drinking, and she was sure it was more than usual, didn't change anything. At five, after a full day of making calls to clients and closing deals, she trotted into Rollie's office, heart thudding and muscles tense.

The tight leather of her shoe dug into her bunion, and she dreaded getting up from the stool and walking ten blocks to the train station. The oxblood T-strap heels had been uncomfortable when she tried them on at the department store. Oxblood T-strap heels. That's what the clerk called them. It seemed like a hideous name in the blur of liquor. Everything about the day seemed hideous. The fine hairs on her arm bristled as the scene replayed in her head. The projectionist was a sadist, bent on revealing all the gut-punching action in Technicolor.

Rollie steepled his fingers together. It was the slick, smooth pose of a snake about to strike.

"Tori, I think we both know your work has been suffering."

She glanced up from the hangnail she'd been flicking back and forth, but she couldn't look directly into his cold, reptilian eyes. They were blue but not a shade found in nature. It was a peculiar, manufactured blue, and she could see the translucent line of the contacts against his eyeballs. It made her shiver.

The fluorescent bulb that stretched above Rollie's desk pulsed in her head. Interrogation? Was he waiting for an admission of guilt? She pressed her fingernails into her palm and refused to admit to anything.

"I just don't think we can afford to keep you on the team anymore," he said. "I'm sorry."

Breath huffed from her lips, and she shook her head.

"C'mon, Rollie. I've done amazing things for this brand. Last year, revenues were up seventeen percent. You know that was my win."

The words, rehearsed over the past week, didn't even convince her.

He held up a finger.

"I'll give you last year's win, but profits are down six percent just this quarter. And it's not just that. McAuley over at Tesco complained you were drunk—I believe the word he used was 'shitfaced'—at last month's client meeting. He said the smell of alcohol radiated off of you."

She couldn't fight it. She *had* been shitfaced. Vodka and tonic, if she recalled correctly since it was one of her favorites, but there had been so many drinks since then, she couldn't say for sure.

"I'm sorry," he continued. "We can't risk losing Tesco, and quite frankly, I think upper management is seriously concerned you could cost us more big clients."

A long, low sigh escaped his mouth, and he leaned forward.

"If it's any consolation, I fought for you. I told them you were one of our best VPs. I even told Anderson you'd been having a tough time since ... since the accident, but it's out of my hands."

There were other words exchanged. The particulars had drowned themselves in half-priced tequila shots hours ago. She remembered leaning over his desk, fists clenched, spittle flying from her dry lips as she yelled obscenities, but the specifics were hazy. A vein throbbed at her temples, and Stevie's neon beer signs burned her eyes.

It was over. The screen flicked to black.

Stevie's was not her regular place. But it was like choosing the hospital closest to you when you've hacked off a thumb in a different city, and you need to get treated right away. It was her triage center.

Her phone bleated, notifying her that yet another Nosy Nancy was looking for some dirt after Rollie brought down the axe. She squeezed the power button, toggled it off, and suppressed the urge to throw it across the bar. No one was particularly concerned about her welfare, but in the marketing game, when folks got shit-canned, it made for the juiciest gossip.

The thought that swirled at the edges of the liquor blur, repeating again and again, was that she was one of those assholes. Stories she'd shared hours ago with her colleagues over cocktails at the bar, gurgled to the surface.

That joke she'd made to male clients about Briana Gilmartin over at the DMS Group. That she had callouses on her knees, and that's the only way she'd made it up the ranks to VP. Dressed in Armani suits and drinking eighteen-year-old Glenlivet, John Errington and Sid Howard puffed Cohibas, laughed, and signed a seven-figure contract for Tori to handle their TV, print, and digital campaigns over the next two years.

She knew full well it was a lie. Briana was a gutsy, determined woman, a woman a lot like herself, who had clawed her way, victory-by-victory, client-by-client up to vice president. Just like she had. But the men told jokes, too, about their assistants, their mistresses, their wives. It was just business. Nothing personal. If she had to throw a few other women under the bus to secure some accounts, they were just collateral damage in a game they all had to play. After all, she'd reached a position of power. Other women would benefit from that ultimately.

If she'd been sober, really sober, she might have bought it. Alcohol was truth serum, and it told her this was a load of bullshit. Tears spilled over the rim of her eyelashes, and she knew they'd tell stories about her. She was a prime cut for the gossip grinder.

Sweat gathered at the back of her neck. A breath caught in her throat, her head buzzed, and her eyes sagged. She closed her eyes and saw the outline of a cheekbone and the glimmer of lamplight against glazed eyeballs. The apparition was almost always on the other side of her eyelids, waiting for her. A tangle of matted hair stretched out around the head. The form, outlined in gray, folded itself at the waist and sat up. A set of arms pressed against the asphalt. The form stood upright. It wavered there for a moment before darkness enveloped it. Tori's knee jumped to slam a brake that wasn't there.

Something thick and wet slid down the girl's face. It oozed and plopped against the sparkling street.

She clutched the edge of the dampened bar. Air left her lungs, and she gasped to suck it back in. Her jaw dropped, and her eyes bulged as she struggled to breathe like a fish flopping across the shore. The room flipped backward in a smear of lights, squeaking stools, and muffled conversations around her.

Her face smashed against the fieldstone, jarring her vision. The stones felt cool against her flame-hot face, and she lay there, a defeated serenity enveloping her.

Something orange caught her eye, and she mistook it for a late-autumn leaf that must've fluttered in with one rummy or another. A monarch butterfly waved its spotted wings back and forth, beckoning her.

Wings folded, it slipped effortlessly through a crack in the fieldstone. Tori reached out a hand, pressed it against the stones, and pulled herself across the floor. She closed an eye and held it up to the crack but saw only an abyss of black below. Her body slid into it, as if pulled by a magnet, and she found herself barreling into this chasm. A set of wings vibrated in her periphery.

A smell, something coconutty with hints of baby oil and a vague tinge of lemon, burst forth. She inhaled sharply and considered what it might have been. Coppertone! And maybe the Sun-In her mom used to spray in her hair on beach days.

CHAPTER 2

She was the Coppertone girl, parked in some sand trench on a Cape May beach, scooping up saline mud pies and plopping them into messy piles at her dad's feet. Her hair was in a ponytail, and she wore her very first bikini, acquired after a lot of begging and whining. It was hot pink with white and blue stripes across the top. Mom wore a white crocheted bikini and pink hot pants, baby oil smeared all over her legs in the hopes of getting just a little tanner before they had to head back up to New Hampshire. Tori had asked if she could do it, too, but was ordered to use the sunscreen instead. It was only SPF 15, so she'd get some nice color anyway.

Dad, hat arranged over his face, can of beer clutched in his hand, already smelled like a Budweiser factory. Alcohol percolated from his pores as the sun coaxed out the poison he'd suckled down all afternoon.

"Doris," he croaked somewhere beneath the floppy hat. "Grab me a sandwich."

Mom plunked down the bottle of oil and wiped her hands on a towel before opening the cooler and fishing out a turkey on rye. She handed it over. He smacked her on the ass as she returned to her beach chair.

Sweat matted Tori's hair to her face, but a gentle breeze made her crane her neck and relish the sweet ocean air. Seagulls cawed at each other, fighting over a sand-coated potato chip and pecking at cigarette butts.

The sun glinted off the ocean. The beauty of it, the pure ecstasy of being there, in the salty, sweat-soaked, sun-drenched air, where the sky and water were the same blue, made her never want to go home. They could just live here like this. The Garretts of Exeter, N.H., could leave behind their mid-century ranch with the peeling yellow paint and the oil-stained driveway and the fights that grew louder and louder as Tori tucked herself up into the covers at night. They could leave it all behind and become the Garretts of Cape May, N.J., a family of happy, laughing people who smacked each other on the rear and got each other sandwiches under a periwinkle sky and smooshed their fingers into wet sand. Those nights she and Mom sat, nibbling cold dinner with their stomachs churning, wondering what might have become of Dear Old Dad were over. Dad was right here. He wasn't going anywhere.

It was perfect.

So perfect that a monarch butterfly landed on her finger and sat there for a moment, resting its wings. Had it been on a long journey? Maybe it had come all the way from New Hampshire to tell them it was okay if they stayed forever.

The wings separated and closed again and again like breathing. After a moment, it took flight, struggling at first to catch the wind. Once it was up, it fluttered off into the sun, brilliance upon brilliance.

"Hey, Tori, babe?"

The muffled croak made her jolt up from her bucket and shovel.

"Baby, go get Daddy another beer, would ya? This one's gotten warm."

He sat up on his elbows, let the floppy hat fall forward, and slugged down the tepid remains of his beer. His mayonnaise-colored belly was round and looked strange as the hub for stick-thin arms and legs. Tori thought he looked like a skinned potato with toothpicks poked in.

Mom's face flushed. Her eyes flared with anger, and she snapped, "That's about enough, don't you think? You're getting our little girl to fetch beers now, are you? She's nine, ferchrissakes."

He crushed the empty can against his kneecap and tucked it into the sand. The hair on Tori's arms stood on end as she braced for impact.

"I don't see what you're getting all worked up about. I'm just asking her to grab me a cold one out of the cooler. It's not like I'm asking her to tend bar. I'll get it my damned self if it's such a big deal."

"Don't you think you've had enough? We've been out here four hours, and you've already finished a six pack."

The final can in the cooler spritzed and cracked as Dad pulled the tab.

"Hot day. What do you expect? I guess you'd be happy if I died of thirst."

Tori felt the eyes of the other beachgoers on her. It felt hotter than the sun itself. She stood up and marched across the sand, down to the pier at the end of the beach where the sea smashed itself against the black rocks and sprayed her baked skin with its cool mist.

Beneath the pier, a couple of boys only a few years older than she puffed cigarettes and swore.

"Hey! Hey, you! Up there!"

One of them pointed at her and gestured for her to come down. She shook her head.

"Aw, c'mon sweetheart. You're looking fine enough to eat in that bikini."

She crossed her arms over her flat chest encased in the rubbery, pink fabric, feeling more ashamed of her body than ever and wanting to hide.

The other boy barked and howled like a dog. Tori's face burned with anger and humiliation, and she ran, arms wrapped across her ruffled bathing suit. Footfalls swooshed behind her in the sand. One of the boys trailed her by a few feet. His blond hair puffed up and down as he neared. The other climbed the hill that abutted the pilings.

They charged at her heels, and she jolted forward, determined not to let them touch her. Her thighs burned as she sped past bewildered tourists. She shoved a hefty man in a blue fisherman's hat to the side, and he stumbled to the sidewalk. She would've stopped to help him up ordinarily, but they were so close, she could feel the whoosh of the air from their arms pumping. Her bare feet smacked the boardwalk. A splinter lodged itself into the meat of her heel.

"Aaaroooo! Looks like fresh meat, Paul. Whaddya think?"

"Could be. Only one way to find out. You gotta taste it."

Tori's heart lodged itself into her throat. She padded down a short stairway and darted between cars lining Beach Drive. Brakes squealed. The sun radiated mercilessly upon her like some cosmic laser beam. All the moisture left her throat.

In her mad escape, storefronts blurred by. A tall, bearded man emerged from a comic shop and held up a meaty hand. Sneakers slapped against pavement, and a deep voice boomed, "That's about enough of that."

Tori ran a dozen feet past the man but turned to see what had happened.

The towering man bent at the waist, hands on hips, face purple with rage. Spittle flew from his mouth as he yelled at them. The boys, shaded now by shop awnings, seemed far too soft and innocent to be potential rapists. They nodded and walked back toward the boardwalk, hands tucked in their pockets, the slump of defeat heavy upon their shoulders.

Tori's lungs burned, and she stood with her hands on her knees for a few moments before trudging back to the shop. The bearded man crossed his arms over his chest and watched the boys scamper back to their hideout.

"Thanks," Tori huffed.

The man turned to her, as if noticing her for the first time.

"Oh, it's nothing. They've been harassing girls all week. Probably some losers from the city who came down here to cause trouble. Don't you worry. I keep my eyes out for thugs like that. Name's Chris. Chris Silver. And you are?"

She liked the way he said his name. First, then first and last.

"Tori. Tori Garrett."

He held out a hand as big as a bear's paw, and Tori shook it.

"Well, nice to meet you Tori Tori Garrett. You ever need to get out of this heat or if you just want some comics, you come on by."

He squinted and tilted his head from side to side and said, "You look like a *Wonder Woman* kinda gal. I think we still have some copies of number three-hundred. I'll put one aside for you. And, hey, watch out for yourself. You want me to walk you back to your parents?"

Chris Silver had a glint in his eye that suggested he understood more than he let on.

Tori nodded. She didn't want to be alone.

"Well, c'mon then."

He craned his head back into the shop and muttered some

instructions to the clerk behind the counter. Then he offered Tori the crook of his elbow. She took it, and the two strolled down the sidewalk. Her feet burned as they crossed the asphalt.

"You okay?" Chris Silver asked.

Tori looked up at him and nodded. Cars stopped to let them cross to the boardwalk, and she felt like a queen being escorted by her king. He smiled and waved at the drivers, and they looked at him like he was the most important person in the world. She clutched his arm a little tighter.

They marched across the boardwalk and into the gritty quagmire of beach. Mom sat, back turned to Dad, watching the tide roll out and the sun waver in an orange haze as it hovered mercilessly above.

Crushed cans littered the sand near Dad's striped beach chair, and the embarrassment of her father's drinking problem burned her cheeks once she realized Chris would see it.

"I'll find them. You can go now. Thank you for your help," she blurted, so afraid he would judge her for her parents.

A smirk lifted at the edge of his lips.

"You got it, kid," he said. "Don't forget to come in before you go home for that *Wonder Woman*."

He turned and walked away. She watched him until he was out of sight and turned to face the frozen chaos of her parents' crumbling marriage.

CHAPTER 3

Tori's cheek stung, and her eyes snapped open. A snake coiled around a staff hovered just above her face. A low voice spoke to someone else in the room, but she couldn't make out the words.

"... coming. round. Okay, back off. Give her some air."

Faces blurred into focus and slowly moved into the background. Light jabbed her eyes. She squinted and pushed herself onto her elbows. A man with a wispy mustache moved the flashlight away.

"Hey! Knock that off," she said, holding the back of her hand up to her eyes.

"Welcome back," the mustachioed man said. "We should get you over to University Medical."

Tori lifted her knees up and shoved herself off the floor. The man in the blue uniform clutched her by the armpits.

"I want to go home," she said, her voice small and hoarse.

"You're very sick," the man said. "You need medical attention. You could have alcohol poisoning."

He said more, but the words melted into the ether as she gazed past him, beyond the crowd of scruffy-faced men, to the orange butterfly climbing its way out of the chasm in the floor. Its wings were folded together as it struggled on tiny, black legs to escape. Then it flapped a few times and flitted out the open door into the bluster.

She snapped back to the man chattering away in front of her.

"I have to go home."

She grabbed her purse from the bar and stumbled on legs that felt heavy and cumbersome.

Her cheek throbbed in the cold. She put her fingers to it. It felt warm and swollen, but there was no blood when she pulled her fingers back. Her hair whipped. Trees encased in wrought iron jutted up around her. Buildings towered over her, and she swung herself into a circle, trying to orient herself toward the train station. The streets to the right crested up into the belly of the city. To her left, trees rattled and swayed in the brutal Hudson River wind. She made a left and then a right until she saw the hulking train station in the distance.

The icy, stabbing squall bit at her eyes, and tears trickled over the lash line. The Hudson heaved and rocked in the wind. Manhattan glowed in the distance, judging her.

Bitterness gurgled in her throat, and chunky sludge crept up. She swallowed, and it burned on the way back down.

A girl with purple hair ran up to her, frantically waving her hands and screaming about her shoes. Tori dusted by her, shoulders tense, turning once to watch the dejected outline in the dark before she trudged toward the train station entrance.

The ache in her head jackhammered between the jarring wind and the street noise. A horn blared at the construction equipment blocking River Street. Some guy in a Lexus jabbed his middle finger out his window to show his extreme displeasure at the stalled traffic. Tori darted across, clutching her Versace blazer up to her neck. She clonked down the sidewalk on screaming feet. Just one more block to the train. She repeated it over and over in her head. One more block.

A spray of brown-red splattered the asphalt outside the taxi stand. Pigeons strutted and cooed around her, and she froze, fixated on that horrid, red blast. It couldn't be. It had to be paint. Or maybe some ketchup dried into the crusty ground from some careless street vendor's cart. That gash spilled blackened puddles onto the crosswalk. She saw it all in reverse and jumped when she watched the wide-eyed, dewy face dash against her windshield.

A shoulder smacked into her back, followed by a "Watch it, lady."

She creaked forward. Only a block. The green station loomed over her, a passage to freedom.

The loud *ssshhhhh* of trains pulling into the station nearly made her cry out as the pain wracked her skull.

There was a 12:08 Montclair-Boonton line train, the last one before she'd have to spend the night on a train station bench. She trotted to Track 15. The train doors were closed. Her stomach churned, and she screamed, "C'mon! Please, let me on!"

The doors shunted open, and she darted up the steps. The conductor's bulging eyes glared at her beneath his cap. The feeling washed over her that the building could come crashing down at any moment, and this might be her only escape. She darted inside, too concerned about her own survival to focus long the strange-faced conductor's expression.

She frowned. This was an old train with dingy, gray-blue bench seats. It smelled like bug spray and stale potato chips. She was accustomed to the soft, red leather bucket seats, but the skin of her heels burned so much, she flopped down. A spring situated itself against her rear end. She bent, unfastened the oxblood T-strap heels, and slipped them off. A water blister poked up from the bright red flesh at the intersection of her toes and foot.

She stared out the window. The faint outline of her reflection gave way to the flurry of people dashing to catch the last trains of the night. Pigeons flapped disdainfully.

The reflection came into full view, but instead of her face, she saw the girl's face. Her eyelashes framed round orbs, just before the windshield cracked. The car lurched forward, and Tori expected to feel the horrid thump of the wheels rolling over the body. There was no thump, and she realized the train was moving. The sing of metal on metal purred as they moved down the tracks.

"Tickets. Tickets, please."

Tori snatched up her bag and rifled around for her monthly pass. The bug-eyed conductor, a broad-shouldered guy in a chambray uniform shirt, huffed and went to the next passenger. He turned back to her, and his eyes bulged like Louis Armstrong blowing, puff-cheeked, into a horn. A lock of curly hair poked from beneath his conductor's hat. She shuddered at the sight of him.

"Something the matter, Miss?"

Her head jerked side to side almost of its own accord as she plucked the pass from some cluttered corner of her bag and held it aloft. He shuffled off to the next car in search of tickets, clicking his hole-punch all the way.

The train swayed as it chugged along, and she stared out the window, her heavy eyes tracking back and forth across the blackened industrial wasteland, red lights from radio towers blinking intermittently. Her face sagged under the weight of the day. The swampy landscape that looked dreary even on the brightest day was a mysterious shadowland. The animals in the meadowlands preyed upon each other in the night, away from the eyes of commuters and tourists. The building lights faded into the distance as suburbia rumbled into view.

She shoved her arm against the window. Warmth radiated from the vents, and the rocking soon put her to sleep.

The girl was always there, on the other side of her eyelids. Black goo seeped from her lips. Her face rested on a glitter-strewn blacktop.

It started on the train. Much, much earlier, though. Her day wrapped at eight. The bars were already spilling over with midweek drinkers. She might have stopped for a Scotch and water, but exhaustion was already pulling at her. She'd started the week in Palo Alto, and the thought of getting home after midnight held little appeal.

She'd walked past the darkened bars and the subdued *thump-thump-thump* of live music to the train station. The ride home was uneventful. She read about forty pages of a novel she'd been trying to get through, and when the train jerked to a halt at Montclair, she'd gotten out and climbed into her car at the pay lot.

There were probably six cars left, gleaming from the light cast down by the lamps. She maneuvered out of the lot and onto the street, manicured lawns and upscale shops blurring by. Strands of white lights wrapped around the trees of a chichi restaurant called Le Petit Crapaud. Those twinkling strings glowed and hypnotized her weary eyes for, how long, ten seconds? Maybe fifteen? By the time she turned her attention back to the street, a darkened outline crossed in front of her car. Her heart leapt into her throat, and her whole body shook as she jumped onto the brake, pressing all her one hundred and thirty-seven pounds onto the black lever. Tires screamed and the smell of burnt treads rose up around her. The figure came into rapid view in her headlights. That frozen, surprised, struck-dumb expression smashed against her windshield, and she watched the girl roll off and thud onto the crosswalk. The car lurched up and down as it thumped over the body. A warm flood spread across her wool trousers, and a noise like a wounded animal erupted from the depths of her chest.

"Miss?"

Red and blue lights flickered in her rearview mirror.

"Miss?"

A hand pulled her by the elbow out of the car.

"Miss? Montclair, Miss. Your stop."

The bug-eyed conductor stared at her, his focus not entirely direct.

She started, and her body shivered.

"Oh. Sorry."

She stuffed her feet into the oxblood T-strap heels and snatched up her purse. The shoes flopped, unbuckled, on her feet as she shuffled down the walkway and onto the platform.

Rain pelted her face as she stumbled to the parking lot and clicked the key fob to open her Volvo. It looked like some of the clouds might thin out.

She hated being home. Montclair was a small enough town that everyone knew her, just by virtue of the horror that happened last year. Her face had been plastered all over the TV. And she felt eyes on her, judging. She automatically assumed anyone who glanced her way knew what she'd done, even total strangers. Maybe she'd judged herself. No charges had been filed, and she knew people certainly had strong opinions about that.

The booze haze she'd gotten at Stevie's had already dissipated, and she wanted another drink. She reasoned that the alcohol hadn't made her fall off the stool. It was anxiety, stress, the shitty day she'd had. She'd just gotten disoriented and turned the wrong way.

Her throat was dry, and her hands shook ever so slightly, a palsy she'd only noticed in the past month or so. It usually struck her in the late afternoon, but it came and went other times, too.

She swung into the Carriage House's parking lot and sat behind the wheel for a moment. The heat from the vents felt good against her chilled, damp flesh. She killed the engine, locked the door, and went inside.

Paolo dabbed at a spill on the bar and looked up at her with a smile. He adjusted his black tie and tugged on the matching vest.

"Miss Garrett! So good to see you. Vodka and tonic?"

The thought of sucking down another V&T made her throat itch.

"Let me get a Jameson on the rocks."

He turned to fill the order, and Tori scanned the room. Same old Blue Bloods. Investment bankers, lawyers, marketing execs. She put a hand to her throat. She felt out of place here for the first time.

Paolo returned with her drink, and she fished a twenty-dollar bill out of her Vuitton.

"Keep it," she said, and tipped the drink against her lips.

It was sweet and toxic and slid smoothly down her throat. A buzz coursed through her bloodstream almost on impact.

The sensation of being watched made her snap upright in the cushioned stool. A woman in a red headscarf, the kind gang bangers wear, glared from across the room. She knew her face. She knew it all too well.

CHAPTER 4

Hot rage rippled over Carla Perez's flesh. A set of blue eyes met hers and hastily darted away. She pressed her hands against the table, dampened by the seven-dollar Corona she'd nursed all night long as she waited.

She strode across the room. Her chair screeched on the tile floor and almost upended as she charged forward.

Victoria Garrett turned to her drink, pretended the two hadn't made eye contact, and chatted with the bartender. Her nonchalance was no matter. Carla had waited too long for this. She'd made the long bus ride to Montclair from Newark almost every week since Lexie died. She observed at first, desperate to know if her child's death had made any impact whatsoever on Victoria's life. Her poor baby had been accepted at NYU and would've started next year. She would've been the first person in the Perez family to attend college. Perhaps Carla had hoped Victoria would drink herself into her own grave. Still, she had a suspicion that what she really needed was a confrontation—maybe even a fight.

She slammed her hands against the bar, and Victoria jumped and turned, spilling her brown drink all over her designer suit. Those glass-blue eyes, vacant and dumb, stared, stricken with absolute dread.

"You know me?" Carla asked, her voice gruff.

Victoria set down her half-empty glass.

"I don't want any trouble with you," she said. "Just leave me alone."

Victoria clutched her purse, and Carla blocked her exit.

"You are gonna to listen to me, you bitch!"

Carla snaked her head into Victoria's face. Hot breath scented with sour liquor fanned from the woman's mouth. It didn't surprise her; she'd watched Victoria drink until she wobbled out the door week after week.

Victoria eyed the bartender, who seemed to be considering his options.

"How does it feel to get away with murder?" Carla asked, her volume at full-blast.

Pain spread across her chest. A lump built in her throat. Victoria mumbled something and pulled her purse close to her body. Tears blurred Carla's eyes, and she brushed the droplets away with the back of her hand.

"My daughter *died*, and you walk free, living life like nothing ever happened. I just want to know how it feels. How does it feel to feel nothing?"

Her voice cracked, and her throat burned with the rawness of her anger. She felt the weight of the stares on her. A few people brushed by her on their way out the door, their haste a window into their discomfort.

Victoria wouldn't make eye contact with her, as much as she tried to coax it.

"I ought to beat the living shit out of you," Carla growled. It was a threat she'd tucked aside, something she'd never act out but couldn't quite hold in any longer.

Except that her fist balled. And she pulled it back. It flew forward before she could cool the bubbling cauldron of hatred she felt.

Victoria jagged out of the way, and Carla brought her fist back and stared at it for a moment, unsure if the action had been voluntary at all.

Carla put her palm against her face. It felt dry and hot. She pulled the cracked leather strap of her purse tight against her shoulder and scurried out of the Carriage House.

It was cool outside. The rain had subsided, but it left the streets slick and shiny. She walked over the manicured landscaping to the sidewalk.

As she walked, she wondered what would've happened if she'd actually hit the woman who killed her daughter. Would she be in a police cruiser right now, heading to county jail, or worse? Her insides squirmed at the thought going through with the act of violence. The vision of the khaki-clad douchebags trying to pull her off of Victoria flitted through her head, and the idea almost amused her.

She'd been watching Victoria for some time now, checking to see what her life had become after the accident, to see how she could live with herself. It had become obvious that she lived with herself by drinking to the point of annihilation almost every night of the week. Maybe that quieted the guilt. But it didn't exonerate her, not by a long shot. And the fact that she could simply drink away the pain fanned those angry flames.

Each time she watched her sitting, legs crossed, at the bar, tossing back shots with her friends, laughing, living, she felt heat rise from her collar. Maybe she regretted not beating the shit out of her, but would that have brought Lexie back? Of course not. Justice had not been served. She knew all things the police claimed. No alcohol involved, which she doubted highly since the woman drank like a fish. It was a tragic accident. If it was so fucking tragic, why was Victoria Garrett able to move on with her life like nothing ever happened? She sucked in her breath. The searing heat that accompanied her desperate desire for revenge skimmed over the surface of her flesh.

The yellowed plastic enclosure of the bus stop dripped from the night's rainstorm. It was illuminated by an anemic streetlamp. Carla stood under it, inhaling piss and the ghost of someone's B.O.

Steam rose on the asphalt as Jaguars and BMWs hummed down the boulevard. The NJ Transit bus sputtered and groaned a few blocks away. The stink of burning oil intensified as it drew near.

The interior lights beamed as it whirred to a stop in front of Carla. The doors hissed open, and she climbed up the steps, inserted her fare, and turned to find a seat. Most of them were occupied by slumped, dark-complected people, hoods pulled up, huddled against the chill. Some slept. A child fidgeted in a stroller, her mother rocking it back and forth as she scrolled through her phone.

Carla sat next to a rotund black woman who smelled like artificial gardenias. The odor made Carla's head throb. She pressed herself against the window and watched the mini-mansions of suburbia roll by. The stone and brick façades of old money were spotlighted against the dark. A lawn jockey, painted white in a half-hearted attempt at progressiveness, stood guard, lantern aloft, in front of a winding stone driveway. The message was still clear. Classicism was alive and well. The residents here used people like Carla as hired help. People with last names like Perez and Washington and Singletary and Ramirez cleaned their toilets and raised their children. People like Victoria Garrett rode on the backs of people like her.

The elaborate homes and manicured lawns gave way to multifamily rental homes and, soon, those gave way to graffiti and subsidized housing projects. The bus wound through the steel and glass of the business district into the gritty, desperate landscape of the inner city. It jerked to a halt at a dimly lit bus shelter. Carla grabbed her purse and shuffled past the floral-scented lady next to her.

She pulled the collar of her coat close to her neck and walked into the drizzle. The wind whipped her hair into a thick, black tangle.

Shadowed figures spoke in low tones. They tucked into doorways, backs pressed against brick, making illicit deals. Carla walked on, looking for number 17.

The West Indies Soul food truck hummed and sizzled. The aroma of cumin, cayenne, and coriander melded with the succulent juices of pork and beef. She used to stop all the time for gumbo or jerk chicken. Used to. All food was tasteless now. It had been that way since Lexie died.

The thought flashed of her child beneath the night-blue, frost-coated ground, tucked into a bed from which she'll never rise. Anger roiled anew. The wind gusted, and the chill tempered the fury that always simmered, just below the surface.

Number 17 was nestled into a dirty alcove that abutted Rai's Market, which was now dark and barricaded by a metal gate. The door, once white, was spattered with mud. Carla pressed the dimly lit buzzer.

"Yes?" The voice crackled through static.

"Miss Tanuja? It's Carla Perez. Can I come up?"

There was a grinding buzz and a click, and Carla pushed the door open. She walked up a dingy staircase. The foyer smelled like curry and mildew.

Tanuja's apartment was separated from the rest of the multifamily house with a set of French doors. Lights glowed through frosted glass. Something *clacked* on the other side, and one of the doors opened.

Tanuja wore an orange wrap around her hair, paired with a white dressing gown. It provided a stark contrast to her deep brown skin.

"Well, come on then," she said, her thick West Indian accent chopping at each word.

She pushed her wire-framed glasses up onto the bridge of her nose and gestured for Carla to sit anywhere.

The apartment was quiet. Strings of lights cascaded from the archway to her dining room. A golden Shiva statue gleamed against the votives of a Diwali display on an oak table. Diwali. Tanuja explained it briefly once, and Carla remembered it had something to do with good and bad, though the details were fuzzy.

"What's troublin' you? What is it you need, honey?"

Carla put her purse down, clasped her hands together, and sat on the threadbare sofa lined with an intricately patterned throw blanket. She felt the hot tears coming up in her eyes, and she rubbed them away with the back of her hand.

"Revenge," she said. "I want revenge against the woman who took my baby from me. Is there some way? Is there something I can do to put her through the hell I go through every day?"

Tanuja's forehead wrinkled.

"Revenge is a tricky thing, Carla. Sometimes, when you hurl shit at someone, you get some on you."

Carla considered this for a moment, and then realized she didn't care. The cosmic ricochet wouldn't matter at all.

"I'm prepared for that. You said there was a way. Before. Right after ..."

Miss Tanuja sat and wrapped an arm around Carla's shoulders.

"Yes. There is a way. You have to believe in it, though."

At this point, Carla would've believed that the Tooth Fairy could come flapping down to take a hit out on this bitch.

"Are you familiar with the *bhoot*?"

"Boot? Like for your feet?"

"No, no. Not boot."

Tanuja looked at the ceiling for a moment, perhaps contemplating the best way to explain it.

"Spirit. Soul. Ghost! Yes, ghost. Something similar to that. Do you believe someone can be haunted?"

Carla nervously licked her lips. She didn't want to admit that she saw things, especially at night when the house was graveyard silent. It wasn't like her teenage daughter flopped down next to her in bed, but every now and then, a wisp would appear. Something out of the corner of her eye would flit by like a puff of smoke. She'd turn to see what it was, but she could never catch it.

"I believe a spirit can be directed, *compelled* to haunt," Tanuja continued. "Lexie for instance. Often, people who die in a tragic way, their spirits are prevented from moving on. Do you believe she's restless?"

Carla pressed her lips together and felt the tingle of tears build.

"No," she said. She knew where Tanuja was going with this, and she didn't like it. Tanuja must have sensed it because she shifted in the cushion next to Carla and pulled away.

"What do you know about this woman? You need to focus all your energy on this person. You can manipulate really *any* spirit to do what you want it to, but ... just be careful."

Carla pulled the phone from her rear jeans pocket and it lit up in the lamp-dimmed room. She scrolled through the photos and showed them to Tanuja. There was an entire folder of pictures she'd snapped of Victoria Garrett at the bar. Sometimes, she was drinking alone, propped on elbows, sunken down into her drink. In others, she was laughing with friends, a shot glass in one hand, her head thrown back.

"I know she's a drinker. A drunk. And that's where I'm going to hurt her. Drunks build up a tolerance, don't they? The more they drink, the more they have to drink, isn't that right?"

Tanuja shrugged and nodded.

"That's what I've heard. I've never been a big drinker myself, so I don't know firsthand, but that sounds right."

"So, what exactly do I do? Just some incantation? Recite some rhyming bullshit?"

Tanjua looked over the thin rims of her glasses and pressed her lips into a frown.

"If you don't believe in it, you're wasting your time—and mine for that matter. You direct all your energy to imbuing her with the spirit."

A smirk worked its way across Carla's face.

"Yeah, I can do that. Let me ask you something. How powerful is this ... *bhoot*? What can it do, exactly?"

"Terrorize. Haunt. You can compel it to do a number of things, but it's not some all-powerful entity. It has limitations. It won't go near water, for one. A lot of what it can do depends upon you."

"Thank you, Miss Tanuja. Thank you for everything. You were always so nice to me and Lexie. I know if she was here, she'd thank you, too."

She stood, and Tanuja followed her to the door. The older lady pulled her in for a long embrace, and as Carla tiptoed out the front door, she knew it would be the last time she saw her friend.

There was a bracing wind when she moved back outside. Her hair lashed around, and she tucked her hands into the pockets of her Levi's.

The water tower glowed, lit from below, and she marched towards it, a soldier on a mission. There was a chain-link fence guarding the tower, but she'd scaled enough fences in her day. She hooked her fingers into the metal links and hoisted herself up. She flipped over the other side and realized with a melancholy chuckle that she wasn't as spry as she'd been all those years ago roaming the streets, jumping fences, hanging with her friends.

It smelled like rust and chemicals. The stairs to the tower were flecked with red and looked unstable, but she didn't care about that now. She clutched the first rung and pulled herself up. The climb didn't take nearly as long as she thought it would, even with the brisk night wind tugging at her.

All Lexie had endured—and the thought of the pain her only child must have endured the night she died—ripped at the still-oozing scab of her heart. She couldn't bear to use her baby's spirit to carry out her spiteful obsession for revenge. It was her last act of maternal care.

At the top, she sat and looked out over the town. Streetlights cast long shadows over the roads. Most of the houses were dark, apart from a few dimly lit windows. And somewhere out there, Victoria Garrett, the evil bitch who destroyed her life, was about to get what she deserved.

She pulled the phone from her rear pocket and flipped through those photographs again. The light was nearly blinding against the black night. She clicked on one photo of the blonde, teeth bright white against her red lipstick. She was hoisting a martini glass in one hand. Carla stared at that photo until it became emblazoned upon her eyelids.

She believed, more than she ever believed in anything, that her spirit would float free, find her, and every time Victoria drank, she'd become sicker and sicker until she would ultimately be destroyed. Carla would take up residence in her body and drain it dry. She wouldn't stop until Victoria was a shell of a human being, a burnt-out husk. Visions of her puking, slobbering, and writhing with otherworldly torture flickered in her head like a movie. It was time.

Her head spun, and her heart thudded as she looked down. She clutched the railing, unsure at first. But there was nothing left here for her. She bent her knees and pushed off, letting go of the railing. The city blurred as she fell. She smiled when she hit the concrete below, jettisoned into a purpose greater than she'd ever known.

CHAPTER 5

Headlights glared and blurred against her windshield. Droplets spattered into view, and the wipers swept them away. Tori's hands ached as she gripped the steering wheel. It was only five blocks. Cars careened past. A horn blatted, and she jerked her Volvo away from the double yellow line.

Vibrations worked down her arm as she swung onto Chestnut Street and then pulled onto Essex. Snot dribbled from her nose, and she pulled her arm away from the steering wheel just long enough to wipe it clean with her coat sleeve. The car juddered onto the shoulder. She wrenched the wheel to pull it back onto the street and swerved into the opposing lane. A pair of lights raced at her. She zagged the wheel just in time to avoid the approaching car. Her heart lodged into her throat, and she swallowed hard. She was so close to home now. Just a few more blocks. Tears welled at the thought of driving more. Her breath hitched. Her chest felt like someone set a dumbbell on it.

She sucked in a breath.

"Okay. Just turn up here. That's all you have to do."

She squinted and pressed herself closer to the windshield as the turn approached. The green street sign came into view, and she maneuvered onto Chelsea.

The guardhouse that kept the riffraff out of The Haven at

Montclair Heights was empty, but she wheeled up to the gate, punched in her code, and the boom barrier lifted.

Her throat was dry, and her hands shook with that old familiar palsy. Anxiety, she guessed. The entire day had been a disaster. Anyone would be shaking if they'd been accosted like she had.

The car lurched forward into the parking lot. A loud crack and a pop sent her bolting upright. The rearview mirror smashed against the brick of the guard house as she drove in.

"Motherfucker!"

She turned the wheel. Wires and glass dangled as she pulled into the parking lot. She found a spot near the entrance to her building, put the car in park, and slumped into her seat.

"You know what? I'm not even going to worry about this shit tonight. I'm too fucking tired."

She grabbed her purse, took the key out of the ignition, and got out. Her legs felt heavy as she wobbled, feet throbbing, to the entrance. Her head buzzed as if electricity sizzled beneath her hair. A clean, sterile hallway led her to a silver elevator. She climbed in and slouched against the mirrored wall. Her knees buckled at the movement of the elevator. She couldn't bear to look at herself.

The elevator dinged, and she stumbled down the hall to her apartment. She unlocked the door and walked into a suffocating silence. Her furniture was outlined in negative in the dark.

"Alexa, turn on the lights."

The space glared against the recessed lighting. Everything was red, black, or white, and antiseptic clean.

She walked to the bank of windows that overlooked the city. Manhattan twinkled in the distance. Low clouds drifted, clearing in spots to display stars. She caught her reflection and put a hand to her head. She'd very nearly gotten her ass kicked, and her hands quaked at the memory of *that woman*. Tori had never met anyone who looked at her that way. The space between her eyebrows had been a deep V. Spittle flew from her lips as she'd yelled at Tori. She put a finger to her chin to dab a long-evaporated droplet at the thought.

Wasn't it enough that her life was falling apart? What did this woman really want from her? Blood?

Acid gurgled in her belly, and the anxious burn that had tormented her every night as she waited for Rollie to can her returned. The silence raised bumps on her flesh. Never mind the visions. Those were harmless nightmares she could awake from and shake off like a fog. This Perez woman was a real threat, so bent on revenge that she might come around and hurt her.

The bottles on the wet bar glimmered. The warm brown of the Jameson's made the saliva percolate at the sides of her jaws.

She walked to the bar and clutched the whiskey. The heavy glass bottle slipped from her grip and shattered against the hardwood floor. A wedge of glass gouged her foot, and she knelt, a constellation of shattered bottle around her. Bits of glass scraped at her kneecaps. She put a bloodied hand to her mouth and sobs built up in her chest. The tears wouldn't come out, but animal noises escaped from deep in her gut, distraught and terrified.

A few breaths in and out, and she stood and went to the sink. The glass tinkled against the stainless steel as she her hands. She pressed her hand against a thick roll of paper towels and left behind a red handprint. She ripped off a few sheets and pressed them against her stinging palm until the blood faded to pink against the white paper. She reached down and plucked the jagged glass from her foot. It left behind a small scrape. The blood had not yet surfaced.

She swept up the mess and ran the back of her hand across her eyes before plodding to her bedroom.

The room was dark, and she didn't bother turning on the light or taking off her clothes before she launched herself into the mountain of down blankets and Egyptian cotton sheets. Her throat tasted raw, like someone stuffed chunks of uncooked steak down her gullet.

Her eyes fluttered shut. A dull, persistent thudding made the nerves inside her eyelids pulse. Gray figures in negative waited to flicker on like a film every time she closed her eyes. Tonight, thick blackness sucked her into an empty pit.

Tori's eyelids were glued together with thick crusts. She strained to open them and rubbed the lashes with her fingertips. They burned in the ghastly whiteness of the room. Horizontal sunlight lined the walls. She threw back the blankets and eased herself upright. She blinked away some of the sleep. An ache ran from the back of her ear all the way down her neck and into the meat of her shoulder. She felt like she'd slept on a bed of gravel. The alarm clock on the bedside table told her it was 3:23. Holy shit. She'd slept into the afternoon.

She pressed her feet against the cold, wood floor and lifted herself to a mostly upright position.

The place was cold and sterile. Sought-after luxury, that's what the brochure said when she'd toured it. And it was a solid improvement over the stuffy one-bedroom in a converted three-floor Victorian over in Caldwell. It was luxurious, all right. It impressed guests, be they clients or one-night stands. But it was not home.

One amenity she hadn't insisted upon was the girl. She lived in the bedroom closet; on the ceiling above her bed; in the bright, wall-sized mirror in the bathroom. She may have even been microscopic in the tiny fibers that flitted skyward when she shook out her sheets. The only escape had been working herself to the point of exhaustion. And drinking herself into a blurred stupor every night. And what now? What would stop her from seeing the young, beautiful girl she'd killed? What would stop the constant pang of guilt that ate her insides more insidiously than any amount of liquor could?

The peach fuzz on Tori's cheeks stood on end as she lifted onto tiptoes to grab a coffee mug. She popped a Keurig pod into the machine and pressed the button. A thin stream of chocolate-brown brew gurgled into the mug. The pungent, slightly bitter aroma steamed into her sinuses, and it eased her headache. The uneasy feeling that she was being watched settled over her like a fine dust.

That bottle of pinot cooled at an optimal temperature in the stainless-steel fridge. She pulled open the door, the gurgle from the coffee maker mocking her, and clutched the yellow-tinted bottle. Then she rifled through a drawer for the corkscrew. She pierced the cork and twisted until the bottle was open. She didn't bother with a glass. She chugged down about a quarter of the bottle, barely tasting the oaky notes as it gushed down her throat. It was afternoon. It's not like she'd sunk to the rock-bottom desperation of morning drinking.

Her nerves were steady, maybe even dulled a little, and she felt like she could make a trip.

She thought about the Absolut locked up tight in the wet bar, but she knew she needed to be as straight as possible to drive. The night before had been a little too scary for her liking.

She moved to the bedroom and pulled the large, red American Standard from the top shelf of her closet. It had been a companion on her endless trips, domestic and abroad.

It would be cold, she knew. Colder even than Northern Jersey, and she dug deep into her dresser for flannel-lined jeans, fisherman sweaters, and waffle-knit shirts she could layer. Duck Head boots would probably see her through the worst of the winter. She'd go for a rugged chic look—L.L. Bean, only classier. The weather wasn't so bad now. Highs hovered in the mid-forties most days, but she didn't know how long she'd need to be gone. She moved faster, eschewing her standard care with folding. Soon, she tossed crumpled cashmere into the bag in close proximity to bra hooks and Velcro.

There was the matter of her lease, but she couldn't worry about that now. She'd figure that out once she arrived. She zipped the American Standard and swung it around on its wobbly wheels.

Her family was in New Hampshire, but going home felt like a bigger failure than getting fired. A forty-five-year-old woman moving back in with Mom and Dad was just about the most crushing kind of defeat she could envision.

The happiest times of her life were spent summering in Cape May, walking in the sunshine, the coconut smell of suntan lotion soothing every worry, the easy breezes lulling her to sleep under crisp, cool sheets. The Bay City Rollers sang about Saturday Night then, and Dad wore rose-colored aviators that took up about a third of his face. His mustache occupied another third. Mom looked like Olivia Newton-John with her feathered blonde locks and shorts that barely covered her thighs, paired always with crocheted bikini tops and platform sandals.

Memories of the place brought her peace, so much that the

knot that had taken up permanent residence between her shoulder blades released. The dull ache in her head eased a bit, and she could envision quiet, off-season days at the beach, huddled against a bonfire, reading a good book and forgetting about the horrors that plagued her mind.

She wheeled the American Tourister to the door and let herself out.

Yeah. Cape May. It might not be the same in the off-season, but it held a lot of promise. All she had here was a vague sense of dread and an itch beneath her skin that shuttled her to the car and onto the highway.

CHAPTER 6

Beachfront inns and cheap motor lodges in pastel blues and pinks along Beach Drive were outlined against a dimming sky. None of the No Vacancy signs were lit. The grungy, cheap motels held little appeal to her, especially since she'd be staying for a while.

She instinctively checked the driver's side rearview and grimaced at the sight of the flopping cables and wires. At the end of Beach, she sat idling and watching the waves break against the black rocks.

The gazebo at the pier stood like a hulking monster in the twilight. She spun the Volvo around at the dead end and jammed it into park. There stood a rusty, grimy payphone, perhaps the last one in the world. A glass coffin encasing it was coated with sand, greasy handprints, and gang graffiti probably etched by some suburban spoiled brat on vacation with his family. She rolled down the window and heard the ocean breathing in and out in the otherwise silent evening. She stepped out and walked to the gazebo, careful to mind the bottle caps and cigarette butts. It was much cooler now, and she tucked her fists into the sleeves of her blazer.

The wooden structure jutted out into the heaving water. Spray leapt up from the depths below. She found a bench at the end, hovering just over the water, and curled herself into the fetal position, knees jutting into her chin. Ice-cold mist flittered against her hair. She shivered, but she didn't mind it. It made her feel sober and awake.

The tremor that typically ran from her fingertips to her elbow was still for now, but it would be back. It always came back, usually around 4 p.m., when she'd taken all the shit she could possibly handle and her boss was shoveling on another pile. Only she wouldn't have to deal with Rollie's shit anymore.

She plucked her phone out of her purse and powered it on. An endless barrage of *bings* assaulted her ears right away.

Tori? What happened? Where'd you go?

Hey, girl. Rollie told me you got fired! WTF? Call me!

Hey, it's Jess. Could you please answer your damned phone? I've been trying to call you all night. I heard you got fired. Let's meet up at the CH and talk. I'll buy you some unemploymen-tinis.

She frowned. So, word had gotten around. Her whole team knew. They weren't really concerned; her shit-canning would just provide some low-level gossip for the vultures that had been hovering over her desk for the past year. The knot tensed up again between her shoulder blades, and she clicked the phone back off, reared her arm back, and chucked it into the spray below. She felt better instantly.

She eased her way back to the Volvo, opened it, and slid behind the wheel. Static crackled on the radio, so she flicked it off. She turned the wheel all the way around and maneuvered back onto Beach.

A B&B with a purple awning caught her eye, so she turned onto Perry Street. There were no cars at any of the meters, so she pulled headfirst into a spot, fed the meter a couple of quarters, and walked up the wooden steps to the purple-painted front porch.

A violet sign with thick gold lettering identified the building as

Seaside House. It wasn't exactly true. Perhaps some of the upper floors may have an ocean view, but it was situated well off of the Beach.

A set of wicker rocking chairs swayed in the breeze, and a flag embroidered with orange, yellow, and red leaves fluttered as she jogged upstairs.

The front door was open beyond the screen door. It creaked as she pulled it and stepped inside.

The interior looked like most of the B&Bs in Cape May. It was probably owned by some elderly lady who'd inherited the place from a long-deceased relative. A curio cabinet lined with Victorian-era family photographs arched up to the ceiling. The foyer smelled like mildew and wet dog, and she considered for a moment finding another place. She shuffled backwards on the purple wool rug when she heard someone stomp against the wooden floor.

"Hello? Anybody here?"

More wooden stomps came from the recesses of the place. There was a large, oak desk just off the foyer littered with papers and beachy knickknacks. The stomps drew closer.

A dark-haired woman in her mid-thirties strutted to the desk.

"Hi there! May I help you?"

"Are you the owner?" Tori asked, a little surprised to find such a young woman inside this matronly, stuffy place.

"That would be me," the woman said brightly. "Amelia Warren. And you are?"

"Victoria Garrett. Well, Tori. My friends call me Tori."

Amelia Warren extended her hand, and Tori shook it.

"Well, nice to meet you. Welcome to the Seaside. Did you have a reservation?"

"No. But I'll probably be staying for a few months. Do you think you might be able to accommodate me?"

Amelia's sunny disposition faded for a moment, and her lips curled at the edges.

"Well, that all depends. How many months are we talking here? Come Spring Break, I can't guarantee anything."

"Oh, I hope to be gone long before next spring. Maybe through the winter?"

Amelia nodded.

"Okay. I think we can work with that. Our off-season rate is $175 a night. I can give you a bit of a break. Maybe $150 a night?"

Tori gritted her teeth.

"I am presently …"

What was the phrase her father used when he'd come home loaded on Wild Turkey after losing yet another job?

"*at my liberty*. Do you think you might be able to get it down even more? I'll help you out around the place all winter long. I can clean and cook."

Amelia sighed deeply.

"To be honest with you, it'd be nice to have some help around the place. Gets lonely here in the offseason. My husband died last year, and the place hasn't been the same. How 'bout we say $200 a week, and you help me out?"

Tori nodded.

"I think that would work." She paused a moment and said, "If you don't mind me asking, what happened to your husband?"

Amelia looked way too young to be a widow, and the revelation troubled Tori.

"Cancer."

The younger woman smiled, but sorrow loomed in her eyes.

"I'm so sorry."

Amelia cleared her throat and dabbed at her eyes with her fingertips.

"So, let's get you set up. The honeymoon suite is empty, and I suspect it will be for the remainder of the winter. It'll give you the most space. It's also the only room with a private bath. I think you'll love it."

She shuffled beneath the desk for keys. The key fob was imprinted with the number 300. The key itself was an antique skeleton key, and it delighted Tori.

"That's so cool!" she said, realizing at once she must've sounded like some stupid teenager.

Amelia giggled, and Tori felt like she'd made a friend—a real one and not one of the fake, gossipy assholes that populated the marketing world. She'd missed the feeling.

"Let me show you up. Do you have luggage?"

"Only one suitcase, but I'll grab it later."

"All right. Follow me up then. Be careful on those stairs. The place could use some work. Maybe you could lend a hand with some of it if you're handy at all."

Tori spent most of her college years fixing up her apartment. She knew her way around a hammer and a drill. She brushed past a flap of torn yellow wallpaper on the first-floor landing.

"Sure. Sounds like a fun project."

The sky was indigo, and streetlamps glowed through the wide picture window at the front of the house.

Three flights up and down a long hallway, Amelia jingled the keys as she unlocked the door.

"Might be a little musty. If it gets above forty tomorrow, you might be well-served to open up the windows and air it out a bit."

The suite occupied about half of the third floor, and Tori was in love. A maple four-poster bed with a gauzy canopy overlooked the ocean. It was probably the only room in the entire house with a full ocean view. A large cherry wood armoire was opened against the far wall, inviting her to hang her sweaters and hoodies. Seashell picture frames in silver and pewter housed more photos of Victorians, all posed stoically, frowns wrought upon their faces.

"Are you okay?" Amelia asked.

Tori noticed her arms were shaking below the elbow. She pressed a hand against her left arm to steady it, but the other arm shook just as violently. Her head throbbed, and cold sweat poured from her temples. She swiped it away with her vibrating palm, and she realized she wanted—no, *needed* a drink. She nodded her head and sucked in a breath.

"I'm okay."

She walked over to the bank of windows facing the ocean and tried to force open the clasp locking them. It wouldn't budge. Her fingers felt thick and clumsy against the metal.

Amelia was across the room in a few long strides, and she reached around Tori, flipped the locks open, and hefted the thick frames up.

The salt air fluttered the thin cotton curtains like ghosts swirling in. A pain deep in her eye socket blurred the white cloth, and for a moment, spirits rose up, and Tori staggered backward. Vague features formed in the creases of the curtains, and she could just make out the face of the girl she'd killed. Her skin prickled.

"I think I may go get my luggage now," Tori said, her eyes fixed on the flapping cloth.

That's all it was—cloth. She was being stupid. It was a child's fantasy of a sheet ghost that could do no more harm than the fabric itself.

Amelia smiled and backed out.

"Of course. If you need anything, I'll be downstairs until about eight."

A jarring desire to get out overwhelmed Tori, but she waited until Amelia's footfalls on the stairs faded into the recesses of the house. The wind subsided, and the curtains fell. Sweat saturated the collar of her blazer, and a dry, angry thirst overcame her.

She *clonked* down the stairs and breezed past Amelia's desk into the chill outside. She hefted the suitcase from the Volvo's trunk, hauled it into the house, and struggled against its weight back up the steps.

Inside the intimate sanctuary of the honeymoon suite, she unzipped the bag and busied herself, rifling through designer sweaters and expensive jeans. Panic gnawed at the back of her neck, coupled with the pressure of someone staring behind her. She wanted to look; she felt a lot like a child who hears an alien noise in the night and pulls the blankets closer in the hopes the threat will pass. The silk of a chemise brushed her hand, and it soothed her for a moment. Just enough time to lull her into believing it was all in her head. She turned. The sunken eyes of Victorian ancestors stared from the pewter frames that lined the dresser. Their lips were pressed permanently into stiff, disapproving scowls.

Tori's hands shook as she picked a cashmere sweater from her suitcase and hung it in the armoire. It was a different sensation from the tremors that typically shook her whole body. Her brows pressed together at the center. The contents of her stomach churned. The urgency to get out grew.

Her ears perked, seeking out the slightest noise from downstairs. Dust flitted up from the furniture and sprayed across the sunlit room as she moved. The curtains swayed, and the wind felt good on her skin.

When she heard Amelia stomp to another part of the house, she edged out of the bedroom and stood at the top of the stairs.

Ruffling noises followed, as if someone was shaking out sheets. Her foot creaked against the first step, and she braced her weight against the thick, wooden handrail. The other steps groaned and cracked until she reached the second landing. There, she sucked in her breath and listened again. The clinking of glasses emanated from somewhere in the back of the house, and she continued, each step ratting her out. Maybe Amelia wouldn't care that she needed a drink now more than she ever had before. Maybe it was her own embarrassment. But a horrible, growing maw opened within her, and she had to feed it.

She made it to the front door and gently closed the screen behind her. Her knees wobbled on the porch steps, and her fingers felt numb. She fished her keys out of her purse and got into the car.

She sat behind the wheel, contemplating where she could go. Her hands quavered. Her throat felt like wads of cotton worked up from her guts. The road ahead blurred. She hadn't touched a drop since she left Montclair, but she felt drunk already.

Back in their Orange Crush, sunshine days, Dad would pull her by the hand through Harrington's Liquors. Its floors had been slippery with sand from hundreds of flip-flop-clad folks padding in and out searching for beach day beers or nighttime piña colada rum. Burglar bars covered the windows and obscured the red and blue neon beer signs. A couple smiled and held Newports at the entrance. They were apparently alive with pleasure. That and nicotine.

Dad would drag her past the brown bottles of liquor to the humming coolers in the back. He'd clutch a 24-pack of Bud, tuck it under one arm, and escort Tori to the checkout counter where he'd say, "Go on, honey. Pick out something for yourself." It was usually a Zero bar, but sometimes she'd choose a Payday. It was a ritual that took place at least twice over their weeklong stay.

Was Harrington's even around anymore? It was north of the beach, so she pulled away from the curb and drove ahead.

The landscape of North Cape May had morphed into a suburban oasis of Wal-Marts, chain restaurants, and supermarkets. Harrington's was still there all right, but it was tucked into a strip mall between a nail salon and a ShopRite.

She pulled into the rutted lot and parked. An electric *bing-bong* announced her entry to the store. A gray-haired, bearded man sat behind the counter, puffed eyes glancing over the newspaper. He barely looked up when she walked in.

Bottles lined the shelves. Coolers housed the beer in the back. If her memory served, the layout hadn't changed at all. A green sign told her the gin was down the same aisle as the vodka and the whiskey. A bottle of Bombay would've held her for a week back home. The shiver in the shoulders made her grab a second bottle and a bottle of Maker's Mark to boot.

The old man at the counter robotically scanned the bottles, stuffing them in brown paper sacks.

"That'll be seventy-three twenty-four," he droned.

She spied the tiny airplane bottles by the register and plucked up four nips of Malibu rum, a couple of Stoli oranges, and three Fireballs.

He ran the mini bottles over the scanner and said, "Ninety-six forty-seven."

She passed him her debit card and tapped her foot against the linoleum. He swiped it, handed back her card, and said, "Have a good one," before going back to his paper.

She hefted the large paper sack to the parking lot and picked out one of the Stolis. Under the liquor store's red awning, she twisted the cap and sucked down the bland orange liquor. The alcohol burned her nostrils as the warmth spread across her. The shakes dissipated. She stood in the darkness for a moment, feeling more human. A man in a torn, oil-stained sweatshirt ambled up and smiled at her, the void where his two front teeth should be, gaping into an undulating darkness inside his mouth.

"Getting it done, am I right, sweetheart?"

Pink and silver tendrils slithered out between his lips and slid down his dirty shirt and onto the cracked concrete. A snake wormed its way toward Tori's feet, and she screamed. Fear paralyzed her to the spot even as the snake wriggled closer. Her legs felt numb, as if the tiny bottle of alcohol had incapacitated her. It all looked like a grainy Technicolor film she was watching from behind a glass. It seemed fake until the snake nipped at her shoe, the oxblood T-strap heel. She felt a fang pierce the leather and poke into the flesh of her big toe.

The grubby man laughed, and Tori watched as slithering serpents dropped, one by one, from his mouth.

She tore off for the Volvo, the bottles rattling and shaking against her body. She shoved herself behind the wheel and watched the man wave at her. If the snakes were still there, she couldn't see them. Cold sweat dripped down her back. She licked her dry lips and took a breath so deep, it made her yawn. Had it really happened?

The ride back to the Seaside was a flight from that *thing*. Her knee jumped at a traffic light, and her hip muscle itched to smash the accelerator and blow through it. A film of hot moisture clung to her trousers. She checked the rearview, and a shockwave worked its way from her shoulder blades down to her pelvis at the thought that a cop could pull her over. She wasn't drunk, but there wasn't any hope at all that she could collect herself. She'd just seen snakes come out of a guy's mouth. If that wasn't grounds for being locked up in the looney bin, she didn't know what was.

She drew in a slow, shuddery breath, held it for a moment, and let it blow between her lips. She turned her attention back to the road and two more right turns brought her to the front of the Seaside.

She threw open the door and flung her legs out. The blood-colored shoe caught her eye, and she shoved her knee up to her chest. The leather was smooth where the snake had bitten her. Her toe still throbbed, but there was no evidence she'd been bitten.

There was no delicate maneuvering back into the house. The ordeal rattled every part of her, and Amelia catching her with a stash of liquor was the least of her worries.

Amelia watched as Tori shuffled the bag against her body and huffed up the steps. The awkward eye contact made her move a little faster to the stairs.

Behind the solid wooden safety of her suite door, she clunked the paper sack down on the small writing desk and clutched the bottle of Bombay. She twisted the cap, and it snapped open. The fumes from the gin burned her nostrils. There were no glasses in sight, so she tipped the bottle back and gulped down her medicine. It scorched her throat.

There was a steady breeze coming in through the window. Tori clutched the bottle and plopped herself down on the bed. The mattress was lumpy, but it would do. Another slug of liquor quieted her thundering heartbeat. She blew out a booze-scented breath and watched the white, gauzy curtains flutter against the black sky. Outside, the ocean roared.

She leaned against the plush pillows piled up behind her and realized she was drained. Her fitful sleep the night before had given her a dull, constant headache. The stress of, well, whatever she'd experienced at the liquor store depleted her of any spare energy.

The bright white behind her eyelids gave way to red. It spread in all directions, and she couldn't fight it. The face was there again. The curve of a soft, youthful cheek pressed against clumps of asphalt. Something drained onto the roadway. An eye, deep brown and sinister, flipped open, and the curve of the cheek deepened into a smile. The girl got up, slick black slime dripping from the gaping wound at her temple. She trudged on broken feet to the bed and laughed. The rotten stench of death flowed from her. A movement at the back of the girl's mouth held Tori's attention. It jutted from the throat and inched up between the girl's shiny, straight, young teeth. A snake, pink and silver, rubbed between her lips and fell, wriggling and seductive, at the foot of the bed. Tori struggled to move, but she could only stare as the snake wrapped itself around her leg and slinked up to her face. It reared back for a moment, as if it was going to strike. Instead, Tori opened her mouth and felt the leathery skin slide smoothly inside and work its way down into the depths of her guts.

Something black choked its way up from the girl's mouth. She smiled and breathed, "It's all yours now."

You can wake up, a voice echoed in Tori's head. Her feet kicked, so sure was she that some venomous thing had taken up residence in her sheets.

The curtains waved, the suggestion of ghostly smiles and blackened death's eyes shrouded in the folds and twists of the cloth. A face emerged from the abstract canvas. Was it the girl? No. The resemblance was there. The cheek curved in the same way. But worry lines furrowed the forehead and lines crinkled at the eye sockets. An older relative. Could it have been her mother, the woman who assailed Tori?

There was a term for the mind seeing faces where there were no faces. She searched the memory of her Vassar psych classes for it. Matrixing? Was that it? It didn't sound right.

Logically, she knew there was no face staring at her. Its cheeks were not lifted in a grin that threatened to turn into a ravenous mouth gnawing at her skin. There were no burning eyes, begging for Tori's painful, excruciating demise. It was all in her head.

Pareidolia. The word sprung up from her memory banks.

All that education, all those years of pulling ideas together and learning the ropes of marketing and making a name for herself, none of it changed the fact that a woman was glaring at her from the window. The expression was a mixture of absolute hatred and mischief.

None of her education and experience could explain away the fact that a ghost was staring her down.

CHAPTER 7

Amelia Warren knew drunks, and she could tell she had one on her hands. The smell, sweaty and sour, clung to Tori. She wasn't unclean necessarily. Showers, perfume, breath mints were all well and good, but nothing scrubbed away *that* smell. Amelia would never forget that stench, even if she lived to be a hundred.

Her husband, Bill, hadn't died of cancer. She'd spent his last days at his bedside, but instead of wasting away from tumors eating at his vital organs, his body, bloated and yellow, polluted itself until he was poisoned. His liver failed first, then his kidneys. It might as well have been cancer. It was a slow, painful process that depleted her of all her sanity.

She told everyone who asked that it had been cancer to save face—not only for herself, but for her late husband. His drinking problem embarrassed her, something she never would've said to his face. But the heat of guilt flushed her cheeks when confronted with it, and it was just easier to call it cancer and change the subject. She'd been a great enabler. Instead of fighting him or nagging him, she'd allowed him to drink any time of day, and supplied it to him when he shook so violently, the whole bed rattled.

Perhaps it was fate that brought Tori to her. Maybe this would be her redemption. This time, she could actually save someone trapped in Hell.

It was already bad. That much she knew. Those convulsions she'd witnessed when she showed Tori to her room meant her addiction was raging. She wondered if her drinking led her to lose her job. How had she put it? She was at her *liberty*? Amelia thought the terminology was charming, but that was the thing about drunks. They could be endlessly charming until you gave every last ounce of yourself to get them their poison.

The deal she'd struck would probably hurt the bottom line. Tourists still trickled in, even in the offseason, but she knew she probably wouldn't be able to rent out the honeymoon suite until spring. There might be a stray Christmas wedding, but those were rare, especially for the beachside towns. Still, she felt lonely, even in the height of the season when the No Vacancy sign burned constantly.

The serendipity of it all confounded her. Last September, Bill gave up and succumbed to his demons. And here was a woman, seemingly haunted by the same demons—and maybe more. How much could she spare of herself to save this woman, if it came to that? And would she even be able to? If she'd learned one thing from Bill's slow crawl to the grave, it was that not everyone wants to be saved.

Clunking from the stairs made her snap to attention, as if Tori had heard her thoughts and was stomping down to confront her. The woman stood in the shadows of the landing wearing the same stained pantsuit from the night before, hair tangled into a fawn-colored mass atop her head. Bags puffed beneath her eyes. A large scratch jagged down her cheek.

"Morning. My goodness, did you hurt yourself?"

Tori blinked and floated blankly from the landing to Amelia's desk. She absently put a palm to her cheek, as if she hadn't noticed before.

"It was stinging when I woke up. Probably just scratched myself in my sleep."

Her voice rumbled like gravel.

Tori's eyes widened a moment, and she said, "Is there some place I can get a cup of coffee?"

Amelia smirked.

"Sure. Why don't we go over to Zoë's? I could use a cup myself. It's just a block away."

Tori looked herself over as if noticing for the first time that she was disheveled.

"Let me go change. I'll be right down."

As Tori whirled around, that smell fluttered up from beneath her clothes, and Amelia scrunched her nose.

She pulled her quilted jacket from the antique coatrack by the door and gathered up her purse. The thought crossed her mind that she should get into the habit of locking it up in the bottom desk drawer. She pulled the strap over her shoulder and leaned against the edge of the desk, arms crossed over her chest, until she heard Tori thudding back down the stairs. Gooseflesh rose on Amelia's arms as the woman approached, looking somewhat more refreshed in a red cable knit sweater and a pair of distressed white jeans. Her hair looked tamer. But there was something *off* about her. Amelia shivered and shook her head. She'd already established an opinion of the woman, colored in no small part by her own experiences. She decided she was projecting, and she should knock it off.

The two walked into the cold sunshine. The ocean groaned and breathed. A couple of joggers bopped up and down on the boardwalk. It was cold enough that Amelia pulled the collar of her jacket up to warm the numbing flesh of her ears. She stuffed her hands into her pockets and hunched against the gale. Tori didn't seem to be bothered by the chill. She walked upright, hands at her sides. A terse smile seemed incongruous to the sullen, pensive expression in her eyes.

"So, where'd you come in from?" Amelia asked, perturbed by the quiet.

"Montclair."

"Nice town. My nephew went to Montclair State for a while. Transferred to Rutgers later on."

The smile fell, and Tori just looked impatient, as if this trip was keeping her from something else she'd rather be doing.

They arrived at Zoë's and walked up to the counter.

"I'd like two large coffees," Amelia said before turning to Tori. "Anything to eat?"

Tori shrugged. The ponytailed woman behind the counter had a pen and notepad at the ready.

"I guess a bagel."

"Two bagels, cream cheese on the side," Amelia said.

"It'll be just a few minutes. Sit anywhere you like."

The tables looked out onto Beach. Summer alfresco breakfasts were popular, but the thought sent an involuntary shiver down Amelia's back. They picked the table next to the space heater. The radiant heat gave off the illusion that it was August.

The waitress balanced two coffee mugs and two plates and set them down.

Tori went for the bagel like she hadn't eaten in days. She ripped a chunk with her fingers and crammed it into her mouth. Amelia turned away and sipped her coffee.

"Any big plans for the day?" she asked.

Tori chomped the lump of bagel and licked a dollop of cream cheese from the corner of her mouth. Her eyes were bloodshot.

"Not really. Just going to finish unpacking, maybe check out the town."

"You're pretty late in the season. Some places pack it in after Labor Day."

"Well, where do the locals go? For fun, for necessities?"

"There are a few places. There's a Wal-Mart and a ShopRite up north, off of Route 9. You'll find more of the restaurants that cater to locals farther north. There's the Rusty Nail on Beach, but ..."

She sealed up her lips the moment she mentioned the place. It had flown out of her mouth on instinct, and she regretted it immediately.

"I think I saw that place when I pulled into town," Tori answered. "Local dive?"

Amelia nodded and said, "Some people run on the boardwalk in the mornings. If it's not too cold, I get out there myself. It's a little bracing some days, but the sweat is good for you, right?"

Tori lifted an eyebrow at the topic change.

The two finished up their food. The walk back to the Seaside was uneventful, and Tori seemed to be more alert and less distant. Amelia briefly regretted renting to her and considered locking up a few priceless heirlooms along with her purse. When things got bad enough, Bill had sold some jewelry her mother had passed down. It seemed like it would be nice to have a friend in the house on those lonely winter nights, but Tori Garrett just might be more trouble than she was worth. Better to be safe than sorry, wasn't that what Mom always said?

Tori studied Amelia between the railing slats on the second-floor landing. The woman flitted about downstairs like a butterfly, busying herself with a dozen little tasks that mattered to absolutely no one but her. The urge bubbled up in her to run downstairs and ask for help.

Something happened overnight. The dream—*had it been a dream?*—of swallowing that snake had been the start of it. It wormed through her body even now. It told her things she didn't want to hear. She tried to block it out. It taunted her. *Drink!* It dared her to gulp down the contents of those bottles tucked away in her room. Suck it all down. It said something else, too. Something that froze her blood and made the roof of her mouth sticky. A hushed voice, grim and tinny, said, *Kill her.*

The room upstairs scared her. The thing that spoke to her was angry. Its voice sizzled like electricity. A terror, like approaching the top of a roller coaster, seized her at the thought of going back to her room and listening, alone, to the voice encourage her to drink herself to death or stab her hostess with a carving knife.

Instead, she waited until Amelia flitted to another room and descended the steps. She went back into the bracing cold and headed down Beach toward the gazebo. The cold soothed an ache that throbbed just behind her eye socket. Her hands trembled again, but she couldn't be sure if it was the chill or the palsy that never quite went away.

She crossed Beach and climbed a short set of stairs to the boardwalk. Sand grit settled on her face. The wind played with her hair. Something writhed inside her, just beneath the surface of her skin. It felt like her blood was alive. As she approached the gazebo and the foam sprayed up from the rocks below, the *thing* seemed to crawl up into her throat.

Get out of here! Walk away now!

Was it afraid of the water? Her head felt like someone clobbered it with a hammer, but a smile lifted at the corners of her mouth. Anger roiled beneath the surface of her skin, and that made her happy. She pressed on toward the structure and heard the jangling of a telephone. It was the grimy payphone at the end of the road. The sound rattled around inside her sinuses. She pulled open the sliding door and walked inside. The booth blocked the wind, but she could hear the dim howl just outside. Hearts proclaiming SC+AK and GE+CS and a dozen other initials of couples that had probably broken up eons ago surrounded her. The clatter of the phone grew more insistent. Tori picked up the black plastic receiver and put it to her ear. It felt cold.

Electricity spat and sputtered on the line. A voice, distant and pained, growled, "Get out of here! You bitch! You get out of here right now!"

Tori returned the phone to its hook. Sweat gathered under her nose. The booth shuddered against the wind, a stifling sanctuary from the groaning cold.

She pushed the door open and crossed the street to the splintered wooden sanctuary where she looked out over the edge. Waves rolled in and smashed themselves against the wood pilings. Globs of water came to rest on her face. Angry heat rose up in her again. This time, her stomach heaved, and she lurched forward involuntarily. A gripping pain seized her belly, and she retched into the spray below. Unending torrents of vomit spewed over the edge of the frame. Her sternum spasmed. Her hair clung to her face in sweaty strings. Empty at last, she stumbled back from the edge and clutched a beam. Her body felt depleted and weak. Her knees wobbled as she tried to get out of the shelter.

Hot and desert dry, Tori coughed and felt a lump clogging her windpipe. She tried to clear it, but it remained.

Electric words, threatening and vile, echoed in her head.

Fuck with me, and you'll wish you were dead.

The lump wouldn't clear, and she struggled to suck in a breath. Panic set in, and she clutched the wood, splinters digging into her fingers. She heaved, willing air to fill her lungs. Soon, the landscape rippled in foggy waves across her field of vision. She sank to her knees. Her jaw fell open, and she gasped like a fish flailing against the shore. Down on the weather-worn planks, she panted, taking shallow puffs of air until, at last, she inhaled. A few more breaths, shaky at first, she stood.

She knew instantly what it wanted her to do. Her vision blurred, and her whole body vibrated as she crossed the sand-strewn dead end. She hiked the few blocks to the Rusty Nail, the place she'd passed on her way into town, the local dive Amelia told her about.

There was a neon red OPEN sign, even though it couldn't have been later than ten-thirty. Still, she needed something, *anything* to stop the shaking. She worried that she might encounter someone on the sidewalk who would see her convulsing like this. Embarrassment flushed her cheeks, and she rushed across the gravel driveway and ducked inside.

A butterfly struggled in the gale on its way out of town.

CHAPTER 8

Chris Silver scooped a glob of ketchup onto his French fry and plopped it into his mouth. A red blot dripped onto his salt-and-pepper beard, and he swatted it with a stained napkin. He swiped at the gauze patch on his cheek, paranoid he'd gotten food onto the bandage. Eleven was early for lunch, but he had to be in Wildwood for a comic book convention by three, and boxes of comics, T-shirts, and toys still sat at The Wizard's Realm, waiting to be packed into his Subaru.

The Nail catered to drinkers, and Chris never touched the stuff. Still, the burgers were good, and they had a giant chocolate chip cookie on the menu that excited Chris like nothing else.

The only other person in the joint was a woman who'd been sitting—rather, *shaking*—at the bar when he walked in. She was conventionally pretty. Probably mid-forties. Something about her made him inexplicably sad.

When he came in, she held a tumbler in both hands, unable to stop the quaking. Her drink sloshed onto the counter, and Bracken, the bartender, mopped it up robotically. It was just another day on the job.

Chris pulled another fry through the puddle of ketchup, slurped the dregs of his root beer until the last few drops rattled in the straw, and crumpled his napkin on his plate. He stood and walked to the bar, a few stools away from the woman, who now appeared to have settled down a bit.

"Hey, Brack," he called. "Can I get one of those giant cookies and my bill? I've gotta get a move on."

The burly, blond bartender rubbed the counter with a filthy cloth and nodded without looking up. He lifted a hinged segment of the counter and disappeared behind a swinging door.

The woman looked up at Chris. He smiled. She didn't. He tried not to stare, but something in her pale blue eyes startled him so much, he didn't look away until she turned her head and took a sip of her drink. It bubbled and fizzed. A G&T, he figured. There had been a fog that wisped across her irises, hazy and dull. She was killing something secreted deep inside her, slowly poisoning it. His stomach churned, and he lost his appetite for that cookie just as Bracken bopped back into the bar, crinkling the bag containing his takeout dessert. Bracken dropped it and the bill in front of Chris and walked back over to the woman.

"Anything else, Miss?"

"'Nother vodka and tonic, please."

She was already slurring. He assumed she was at least four drinks in. Pity. She was a lovely woman. A bit young for a romantic interest, but he hated seeing anyone in pain. Maybe his days as a superhero weren't over just yet. He absently pressed his fingers against the bandage, a reminder of the last time he'd leapt to someone's aid. His face burned remembering the incident. It left a scar he'd probably have forever. He wasn't ashamed of rushing to save that woman months ago. He was mostly horrified that he'd been the one taken out on a stretcher. Yes, QuickSilver was back––he never went away. But this time, he'd have to be more cautious.

He fished the wallet from his back pocket and plucked out

enough cash to cover the bill, plus a generous tip for Bracken, who was the only one working this early in the day. He plunked down the cash, then thumbed out a business card.

"Miss?"

The woman looked up, alarmed.

"I don't mean to intrude, but you look like something might be bothering you. I've been through some stuff myself, so if you ever need a friend, here's my card. My name's Chris. Chris Silver."

The woman didn't respond, but she took the card and studied it for a long time, narrowing her eyes as if trying to focus on the words. He turned and walked out, but he couldn't shake her from his mind. He'd fallen into the bottle himself a long time ago, and damn if it hadn't been hell trying to crawl back out.

Chris. Chris Silver. Tori flipped the card back and forth between her index and middle fingers. Could it be *the* Chris? Chris Silver? She searched her memory for the face, but her head fuzzed, and she just couldn't recall what the man who'd saved her all those years ago looked like.

Keyboards set to a faux steel drum *blinged* and *blonged*, and a white-haired man in a blue and purple Hawaiian shirt strummed a guitar and sang about searching for his lost shaker of salt on the stage to an audience of two.

The bartender sidled up to the counter again and said, "Get you anything else, Miss?"

The shaking had subsided. She felt calmer. The buzz that

coursed through her body dulled the incessant sizzle and hum of whatever dwelled within her. Even so, she said, "I'll have one more."

He plucked up a spouted, blue-tinted bottle of vodka and poured, dousing the ice cubes until they cracked. Then he held the glass under the soda spigot until it was filled. He rimmed it with two lime wedges. Tori's glands ached in anticipation at the sight. He set it on the bar and walked away. The drink crackled and fizzed. Her medicine was right there, and her fingers buzzed with the need to pick it up. Her arm shuddered. Still, she clutched the glass and brought it to her lips. The bubbles tickled her nose hairs.

The singer droned on in a key that Jimmy Buffet probably hadn't intended for this song. She was not instantly transported to the Florida Keys. If anything, the fake steel drums and the off-key caterwauling made it seem even more depressing. Trying to fend off the urge to drink in a mostly empty bar in the offseason of a beach resort town was damned near impossible.

It was her own damn fault. So she drank down her medicine, poisoned herself just a little bit more. Her belly ached as she swallowed it, not really tasting the bright, lime flavor. Her throat bobbed as she gulped, and she pulled the glass away empty save for the ice.

She leaned forward and motioned for the bartender to come back. "Who was that guy with the bandage?"

"Chris Silver. He owns the comic shop over on Carpenter Lane. Why? Was he bothering you?"

The word *bothering* puzzled her. That coupled with the white bandage that covered the left quarter of his face elicited a shiver.

"No, not really. Why? What the hell happened to his face?"

A long sigh escaped the bartender's pouty lips. A black lacquer nametag identified him as BRACKEN, and Tori thought it was the oddest name she'd ever seen.

"Guy has some serious issues. He's some self-appointed Superman or something."

Bracken's nostrils flared.

"Anyway, to answer your question, some asshole slashed his face this summer. This tall dude from somewhere up in New England brought his girlfriend here a couple of times. One night, they got into a fight, and he starts beating the shit out of her, so Chris took it upon himself to bring the guy to justice. Stomped right up and stuck his hand out like a motherfucking crossing guard. No lie. The guy took out a pocket knife and ran it across Chris's cheek. Girlfriend left on a stretcher, and so did Mr. Fantastic."

Bracken's expression softened a little.

"He's not a bad person. Quite the opposite. He's too good almost. But he sticks his nose in where it doesn't belong. I think he really believes he has superpowers."

He waved his ratty dishrag. "I've heard rumors about him, but I don't know if any of it's true," he said. He flipped the rag over his shoulder and leaned against the counter on one elbow. Tori noticed for the first time that he was attractive. Not the type she typically went for, but he had potential as a hookup.

The singer mumbled into the mic about taking a break, and the blips and bloops of ELO's *Telephone Line* played over the speakers, tinny at first like the earpiece of the rotary phone her family'd had when she was small. The shudder that had been almost constant for the past two days eased, and it felt like she really was living in twilight, soft and fuzzy and quite unlike herself. Blue days, black nights. No other words could better describe the past year of her life. The music pulled her back to summer in the early 80s when this song played over the speakers at the arcade. She and her parents would eat hot French fries and sip slushy lemonade and walk across the blistering sand to the soft shore. The waves would rock away all the turmoil the family experienced when they weren't on vacation.

The love you need ain't gonna see you through.

It was cheesy, over-the-top, and so out of character, but her heart fluttered as the music rose and he leaned closer.

"So, you new in town?"

She couldn't look him in the eyes, so she focused on the dirt-mottled linoleum floor.

"Just in town for a couple of months. I'm staying at the Seaside."

"Nice place," he said. "Amelia's a sweet lady. Shame about her husband. He was a nice guy. Bit of a character. Name's Bracken. And you are?"

"Tori. Nice to meet you."

He held out a hand, and Tori took it. It felt rough and thick in her smooth palm. Electricity sizzled from the touch, and she felt like she might burst into flames.

"Pleasure's mine. Hey, listen. I get off at five-thirty. Would you like to have dinner?"

A twinge of embarrassment rushed over her. She definitely had a type, and Bracken the Bartender did *not* fit. That type was usually self-centered, professional, and aloof. And the long list of exes veered little from the pattern. There was Jay, her first live-in boyfriend, the one who broke up with her because she was a "fat bitch," his words, not hers. She'd been a size four then. Imagine what he'd think of her now, twenty years later, a massive size eight. He'd probably puke. Fucking idiot. Then there was Peter, the tall Brit who'd been so involved in his late-90s startup that he worked twenty hours a day. She'd grown tired of waiting for the one night a week he could devote to her, so she'd moved on to

Tim, the man she married. She survived more than ten years of his infidelity, neglect, and anger. He seemed to have a never-ending hunger for something that wasn't her. It was a testament to her love for him that she lasted more than two years. So, why were her cheeks flushed? Why was her heart racing?

He smirked uncomfortably as he waited for her response.

"I don't know," she said at last. The fear that she would do something reckless, involuntarily or otherwise, weighed heavily on her.

"Well, could I at least give you my number, and maybe you could give me a call sometime?"

Tori's stomach sank at the thought of her phone sweeping across the ocean floor.

"I don't really have a phone right now."

He raised an eyebrow at her and said, "Seriously? You must be the only person on the planet without a cellphone."

The shudders radiated through her body again. Her gin and tonic melted just a foot away. She clutched the sweaty glass and swigged it. It did very little to stop the shakes.

"It's a long story," she said.

He was already turning away, shoulders hunched up.

"Hey, listen," she called. "Maybe we could go for a walk later. Meet me at the Seaside at seven?"

He paused and turned back.

"Rain in the forecast," he said.

Tori smiled.

"It's only water."

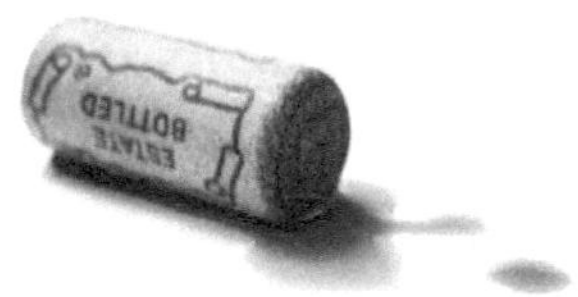

Now more than ever, Tori wanted a bath. She hadn't had one since she left Montclair. She smelled like alcohol-soaked sweat, an aroma with which she'd become deeply intimate. Many a family beach outing, she inhaled it on the breeze from the open car window as her father drove them home from the beach after a day of sitting under an umbrella, throwing back can after can of Old Milwaukee.

Upstairs at the Seaside, she slipped off her shoes and rubbed the red, swollen bunion on her left foot. It felt heavenly. A dull ache behind her eye socket accompanied the foot pain. She undid the buttons of her jeans and folded them on the bed. She lifted her sweater over her head and unclasped a string of pearls and tossed them on top of the jeans. She walked into the en suite bathroom in her underwear and gasped at the luxurious facilities. A claw-foot tub took up about a quarter of the room. A wooden blue vanity topped with more Victorian photos and a few tapered candles stood along the far wall. A pedestal sink offered soaps, lotions, and puffy white towels.

A large mirror sat atop the vanity, and she stared at the reflection. A white mist, ephemeral and faint, appeared just above her head. It was just visible enough to catch her attention. She saw the swirling steam outline of a pair of eyes. The vision dissipated as quickly as it appeared, leaving her unsure about what exactly she'd seen.

Uneasy now, she plugged the tub, selected the lavender-scented body wash, and poured it in. The hot water steamed as it filled the antique tub, and bubbles rose up to a fluffy swell. She unhooked her bra, slipped out of her panties, and sank into the warm, frothy womb.

She felt almost human again, now unsure if she'd even seen

the vision in the mirror, cradled and soothed by the calming scent of the bubbles, lulled into a sense of serenity by the warmth. The ache behind her eye eased. She sank down, letting the bathwater soak her hair and eradicate some of the sweat and filth that clung to her.

The suds popped and fizzed around her, and the subaquatic thrum drowned out everything except for the dulled *bump-bump bump-bump* of her own heartbeat.

Something quivered in her belly and roiled sickly. She bolted upright and her skin crawled at the sensation of ripples sliding on the inside of her flesh.

A long, slow bubble worked its way up from the back of her thigh up to her knee, and it migrated along her hip until it came to rest on her elbow. It slinked around her arm, and she leapt up, sloshing water over the side of the tub. A silver and pink snake poked its head out of the water. Its forked tongue wagged out at her. She threw her leg over the edge of the tub, dragging the rest of her body behind, dripping soap and water in her wake. She watched from the white bathmat as snakes wriggled free from the confines of the froth. They slapped against the tile floor as they exploded from the lip of the tub.

Tori's scream bounded off the walls. It sounded like a roar in her ears. She slipped and smashed her big toe against the tile as she barreled through the door and back into the bedroom. She slammed the bathroom door as they wormed their way across the slick floor.

Shivers rocked her entire body. She stumbled to the other side of the four-poster bed and watched as the serpents snaked beneath the door on a flood of bathwater.

The bedroom door slammed open, and Tori leapt forward onto the bed.

Amelia stood there, eyes wide.

"What the hell is going on?" she squeaked.

Tori gulped in a breath and motioned to the bathroom door.

CHAPTER 9

Chris Silver slammed the trunk of his Subaru shut and lumbered to the driver's side. He buttoned the red cable knit sweater over his Black Lightning T-shirt. The sweater bulged in places where the buttons couldn't quite pull the fabric over his belly.

He flopped behind the wheel, clicked on the radio, and plugged his iPod into the auxiliary outlet. The iPod was his one foray into newfangled technology. It was a phenomenal convenience to carry all his favorite music in this pocket-sized device. He didn't much understand the need for a smartphone when his stupid phone worked just fine. He didn't understand the concept of sharing every aspect of his life on the internet, especially when necessity demanded he keep a lot of his life private. One slip, and the world would know he was QuickSilver, and he didn't want to think about the fallout from that revelation.

Jon Anderson's bright, melodic voice rose up from the speakers, and Chris put the car in reverse and rolled onto the pockmarked road. He put it in drive, and brittle brown reeds by the roadside rustled as the car zoomed past. Even with the windows rolled up, the subterranean smell of saltwater and fish wafted in through the heater vents.

He pulled the wrapped cookie he'd picked up at the Nail from the passenger's seat. He ripped the cellophane open with his teeth and pulled it back. The buttery, chocolatey smell made him chomp off a large section and fill his cheeks with the sweet, chewy confection that melted on his tongue. The Subaru crested a hill. A terrapin dillydallied along the roadway, and he eased the car to a stop just behind it. He parked and shuffled out to pick up the timid, hissing testudo. He carted the little critter to the other side of the road where it waddled into the brackish water. Something fluttered in Chris's periphery, and he turned to see an orange butterfly settle on a broken reed. It took his breath away to see the brilliant color against the drab shades of gray and oatmeal that constituted the marsh this time of year. The lighthouse jutted up in the distance.

He trotted back to the idling car and got in, pondering the orange and black wings pulsing in the bitter wind. Margaret once told him monarch butterflies were a signal that a lost loved one was trying to make contact. He wanted to believe that. He hoped with all his heart that Margaret and Emmy were just stopping in to say, "Hi," from wherever they were now. The thought simultaneously delighted and agonized him. He wondered if it was a sign that they forgave him. The idea brought him no comfort. He didn't deserve forgiveness.

He sucked in a long breath and blew it out, just like the therapist instructed.

"Mountains come out of the sky, and they stand there," he caterwauled along with the iPod.

He pushed down the grief and took the exit for Route 47. Setup started at four, and he was already running behind. He pressed the accelerator a little harder and breezed past browning pines. Soon, the woodlands were replaced with strip malls and chain restaurants.

He maneuvered the car into the parking lot of the Holiday Inn

Wildwood just after five. The hotel had seen better days. The first time he'd attended WildCon back in 1997, the building was fairly new with freshly paved asphalt. Now, the parking lot was a minefield of potholes, and the façade was cracked in places. Greasy-haired men in black T-shirts huddled together in small groups just inside the grimy foyer window. He wheeled into a spot, killed the engine, and walked inside.

A blast of heat assaulted him as he entered. The foyer was neat but dated in shades of cranberry and forest green. It smelled like artificial cinnamon.

Chris recognized a few of the bespectacled people chatting in a small seating area across from the check-in desk. He nodded his greeting and bellied up to the counter.

The clerk, a pretty brunette in her thirties, glanced up from her computer screen and offered him a strained smile that suggested this weekend was going to be her worst nightmare.

"Good afternoon," she said. "May I help you?"

"Yes, checking in. Name's Chris. Chris Silver."

She tapped on the keyboard and nodded as she tracked down the right reservation.

"There you are. You're going to be in room 217. If I could just get your credit card and ID, I'll get you all set up here."

She glanced past him to the congoers coming in and leaned in conspiratorially.

"So, what is this thing exactly? My boss told me there was an event, but I've never seen anything like this before."

Chris chuckled.

"It's a comic book convention," he said. "If anyone gives you grief, you come find me. I'll put them in their place."

He winked, and she smiled, a look of relief washing over her.

"I'll be sure to do that. So, your total for this weekend comes to $242.39."

She swiped his card and handed him two keycards.

"The elevators are just down this hallway and to your left. And if you need anything at all, my name is Jessica. You have a great day, Mr. Silver."

Chris smiled and tucked the key into his back pocket. Around the corner, a cardboard sign emblazoned with a red comic POW! blast informed him that WildCon registration was just down the hall. He followed the corridor to a folding table. A twenty-something guy with a beard that looked like an explosion in a pubic hair factory looked up over the black frames of his glasses.

"Can I help you?" he said in a monotone.

"Yes. Chris. Chris Silver. I'm a vendor."

The youngster rifled through a box until he came up with Chris's nametag.

"You gonna need any help setting up?"

Chris smirked. The kid was implying he was some dead battery who didn't have any juice left.

"No, thanks. I've got it under control. Where's the dealers' room? I just need to know where to pull my car around to unload."

The bearded kid lifted an eyebrow.

"There's no unloading area. You'll just have to bring boxes in one at a time. We do have a dolly you can borrow."

Chris's shoulders slumped.

"What? There's not even a loading and unloading area?"

The guy shook his head.

"Dolly's in the dealers' room in Conference Rooms A and B."

Chris pulled the lanyard with his nametag and vendor designation over his head and walked back into the chilly afternoon. He didn't need a damn dolly. He might have been old, but he was stronger than most people knew.

Still, he started doing the math in his head to determine how many back-and-forth trips he'd need to unload. By the time he reached his car, he sighed heavily and silently cursed himself for being so damned stubborn. He stacked up three boxes of Mylar-bagged comics and hefted them up, his elbows straining against the weight.

Fifteen trips later, he collapsed into a folding chair behind his table, sweat rolling into his beard. He batted a drip away from the bandage on his cheek and adjusted his glasses. Across the expanse of conference rooms A and B, fans filtered in. Dinnertime was over, and folks were coming in to shop before scurrying off to room parties.

Most of the kids were nerds in the most stereotypical definition. Glasses, superhero and rock band T-shirts, frizzy hair, acne. The room already smelled like ass Havarti. That was what Margaret always told him. "This room smells like ass Havarti. Don't these kids ever bathe?"

He chuckled at the memory, and a pang stabbed at his heart.

A tall, thin guy in a Ramones T-shirt walked in, leading a pack of guys who looked like they'd be far more comfortable at a punk club than a comic convention. The smirk on the King of the Turds' face prickled the hair on Chris's arms. The instinct that regulated his hero form kicked in. A jolt of adrenaline followed, so he watched—and waited. He perched on the edge of the metal folding chair, hoping this punk would give him a reason to leap.

The gang walked the circuit of the dealers' room, pausing a moment at Chris's table to look through some comics. The kid in the Ramones shirt gave him a shit-eating grin. Chris scowled.

They exited, but the uneasy feeling remained in Chris's belly. A few customers bought some rarities he had on display, but business was pokey. An hour later, the room closed, and he dragged a tarp over his merchandise and collected his cash in a locking deposit bag.

A guy in a flannel shirt draped over a Hulk T-shirt walked up.

"Chris! Hey, man! Long time, no see. How's it going?"

Chris looked up and smiled. He studied the round face and tried to pull the name from the depths of his memory banks. He glanced as surreptitiously as he could at the nametag.

"Hey, Doug! How's life treating you?"

Doug used to come into the store, back when he lived in Rio Grande. He was almost obsessed with Preacher comics and snapped up every Sandman omnibus as soon as they arrived in the store. It had been a while, Chris reasoned, but he usually wasn't so bad connecting faces with names. Perhaps that punk kid really had gotten to him.

"You heading to any parties tonight?" Doug asked.

Chris hadn't been to a room party in years, but tonight, he felt like some company.

"Sure, why not? Any good ones?"

Doug placed a hand on his shoulder and gave him a knowing look.

"Trisha and Scott have soda on tap, and I heard someone brought handmade truffles."

Chris perked up, and the two walked through the room, passing a mannequin dressed as Spiderman. The costume, torn in places, was far too small for the long, lean mannequin, giving it the appearance of an alien. Chris and Doug looked at each other and laughed.

The elevator was crowded, and Mr. Ramones was in the back, arms crossed over his chest, permanent smartass sneer plastered across his face. Chris returned his focus to Doug.

"So, where are you living now?" he asked.

"I'm down in Delaware now, of all places. Not too far from the ferry, so I get over to Cape May from time to time. The last time I was in town, your store was gone," Doug said.

"Yeah. After Margaret and Emmy died, I got out of the business for a while. But by the time I cleaned up my act, commercial rents on Beach were sky-high, and I ended up renting out a space on Carpenter Lane, over near the square."

Doug nodded sympathetically.

"Hey, next time I'm in town, I'll swing by. Maybe we can walk over to Il Fiorino and grab some good Italian. I'm sure I don't have to tell you that Delaware is a vast wasteland when it comes to Italian food."

The two friends laughed.

The elevator dinged, and everyone stepped off. Chris tracked Mr. Ramones with his eyes. They all walked down a corridor of rooms, many of which had signs on the door announcing some themed party or another. One had a picture of the Tardis with *Dr. Who Fans Unite!* written in white letters. Another had a picture of bees and announced it as a Mead Party. The party Doug was taking him to announced itself as the Dry Oasis featuring homemade truffles. The door across the hall was marked with a large black X. Mr. Ramones walked into that door and shut it before Chris could see inside.

Doug held the door to the dry party room, and Chris followed him, glancing over his shoulder to the room marked X.

A room full of people lounged on the two beds, the armchairs, and the floor, chattering and laughing. Doug hugged the hosts and made his way to the dresser, which doubled as a serving table for the truffles. Doug bit into a chocolate and closed his eyes in bliss.

"Ah, Chris, my man. You have *got* to try one of these."

Chris didn't need much convincing. He plucked up a nut-coated truffle and popped it into his mouth. The crunch of the outer shell gave way to a melty, gooey inside that burst with raspberry flavor. He smiled. It was divine. On the other side of the room, the hosts had set up a soda fountain. He grabbed a plastic cup and wedged himself past the throng of people milling about in the cramped space to get a drink.

Doug was chatting up a woman in a laser cat T-shirt, and Chris suddenly felt his chest tighten with anxiety. The drink tasted too sweet, like it was all syrup and no water. He set it down on the dresser next to the truffles and shuffled through the bodies to the door. It was too much. The noise, the wriggling mob of people. The chocolates were good, but, damn, they weren't *that* good.

The hallway felt about ten degrees cooler. It smelled slightly better. The pressure in Chris's chest eased a bit. A few doors down, he saw Mr. Ramones leaning over a woman, his hand on the wall above her head. She had her arms crossed over her chest, and she was looking down at the stained cranberry carpet. Chris pressed his back against the wall and watched. The woman's lips were twisted into an uncomfortable smile. Mr. Ramones was speaking in a low, deep voice Chris could barely hear.

"C'mon. I promise it'll be fun ... If you get bored, you can always ... my room."

The woman fidgeted and inched backward. She shook her head.

"I'm sorry," she said in a small, high voice. "I don't think so. I promised my friends I'd go to their party."

Mr. Ramones slapped the wall just above her head and growled, "Stupid, uppity bitch! Bitches like you think your cunt is lined in gold."

He leaned in closer and grabbed the woman's arm.

"Let me tell you something. I've had a hundred times you. And you're not even worth the effort."

Chris was across the room in a few steps. He felt the change as he moved. The adrenaline coursed through him, and he clasped Mr. Ramones' arm and twisted it before the boy even realized QuickSilver was upon him. The woman bolted down the hallway and pounded on a door.

"Hey, this old guy is beating up some asshole," she yelled.

Chris smashed the guy's head into the wall and kicked him in the chin when he slumped to the floor. Mr. Ramones looked up, pink spreading across his teeth and terror in his eyes.

"What the fuck, man?" he spat, blood splattering with each word.

"That's not how you treat a lady," Chris huffed.

Mr. Ramones curled himself into the fetal position, and Chris turned to the find the woman.

"Are you okay, Miss?"

Her bottom lip quivered.

"That was fucked up," she said. She seemed to consider what just happened for a moment, and she took a deep breath. "But seriously, though. Thanks for helping me. That guy was a real dick. He was bothering one of my friends earlier."

She turned to look down the hall and leaned closer to Chris.

"If I were you, I'd get the hell out of here before security gets to you," she added with a mischievous grin.

Chris knew she was right. He walked to the elevator, hit the down button, and climbed aboard just as hotel security arrived. The elevator zipped down to the lobby. He went to his car, gathered up his overnight bag, and headed to his room. His muscles ached, and he felt like he'd run a marathon. He was getting too old for this shit.

CHAPTER 10

Amelia shoved open the door and stared as Tori straddled the sheets, hair dripping, eyes stricken with terror. The nude woman motioned to the bathroom door. The room smelled like lavender. Apart from the disheveled woman hunched on the bed, nothing else seemed out of order.

She rounded the corner and opened the bathroom door. Soap bubbles crested onto the floor. The water sprayed and overflowed onto the tile. She shut off the tap, gathered up the guest towels perched on the pedestal sink, plopped them onto the floor, and swirled them around with her feet, drying up as much of the mess as she could.

She went back into the bedroom to find Tori had wrapped the sheets around her body.

"Want to talk about it?"

The terror had not left Tori's face yet.

"The snakes. Are they gone?"

Amelia's eyebrow lifted on its own.

"Snakes? There are no snakes here. There's nothing here. You left the water running, and it soaked the floor."

Tori scampered toward her and got so close, Amelia could smell the hot, burning odor of liquor on her breath.

"They were there. I promise. I saw them. They came out of the tub."

"Just look," Amelia said, the annoyance in her voice impossible to suppress.

Tori peeked over the edge of the bed. Confusion replaced the terror in her eyes.

"I swear to you ..."

Amelia sucked in her breath.

"Listen, I didn't want to say anything, because, hey, it's your life, and I don't want to be that bitch, but do you think maybe you have a drinking problem?"

Her gaze instinctively went to the bottles on the writing desk.

Tori's chin grazed her chest.

"I know I have a drinking problem," she said, her tone even and soft. "I want to stop. Do you know what I see every time I try to stop? I see the face of the girl I killed."

Tears were spilling over her eyelashes now.

"I see a life I took. I relive the moment I got out of my car and saw her smashed against the asphalt. I get to look at it over and over and over ..."

Her voice was wild now, high-pitched and garbled with tears until Amelia couldn't understand the words.

Amelia stood rigid, arms crossed over her chest. She wanted to feel empathy. She really did. Her mind raced back to all those nights she'd cried her eyes out, begging Bill to put the damned bottle down, to knock it the fuck off already and get some help. She knew, more than anyone, how charming a drunk could be because one had charmed her and wooed her and left her all alone.

"I think if this continues," Amelia started, her voice cool, "I'm going to have to ask you to leave my home."

A flicker of icy terror resurfaced in Tori's eyes and dulled again as she realized she had to do *something*.

"Can we at least talk?" she asked.

A shudder of discomfort overcame her, and Amelia said, "Sure. Just put some damn clothes on."

She turned and walked back downstairs.

A short time later, the creaking of the steps heralded Tori's descent. She'd slipped into a cream fisherman sweater, a pair of jeans, and marled cotton socks. Her hair was damp and flowed in loose curls around her shoulders. Funny how the most fucked-up people could look so normal. Amelia shook the thought from her mind. She wanted to be fair and give her the opportunity to explain. She wasn't committing to anything. If this woman continued to make her feel uncomfortable, she was within her rights to make her leave.

Tori sat on the wingback chair across from the desk and crossed her legs.

"Listen, I'm really sorry," she said. "I don't know what happened. I'm not crazy. Well, at least I don't think I'm crazy. Given everything that's happened to me over the past day, maybe I am. Yesterday, I got fired from my job. I was drunk at a client meeting, and I lost my job. And, I don't know, I remembered all my childhood memories from this place, and I just had to run away from my problems for a while. Except for the past twelve hours or so, my life has been nothing but problems."

Amelia set her jaw.

"What about the alcohol? Is it possible you're just drinking more than usual because you lost your job? Maybe that's the root of your problems."

Tori's cheeks glowed red.

"I've already told you. If I *could* stop drinking, I *would*. Only now ..."

She stared past Amelia into the sea behind them.

"Only now what?"

"I don't know if I could even explain it. See, a year ago, when I really started drinking, everything got so much better, at least when I drank. I didn't have the visions anymore. I could almost cope with the accident. It's different now. I see things. Snakes, mostly. And I still have flashbacks about the girl. Only, now I'm having visions about someone else, another woman."

Her shoulders heaved with a big breath.

"You probably think I'm cuckoo for Coco Puffs, and I wouldn't blame you for kicking me out. Hell, if some drunk came into my house and screamed about seeing snakes, I'd probably do the same."

Amelia saw desperation in her eyes, deep inside the blue and green strands of her irises.

"Just, please, give me the chance to get myself together. I won't drink. I won't. I'll just stop."

Amelia had heard those words a million and one times from Bill, and she never believed them from him. She definitely didn't believe them from a stranger.

The sunlight that filtered into the room dimmed, and Amelia noticed the clouds gathered over the shore. A storm was coming. She just hoped she was ready.

Tori was jostled from her plea by rattling from the screen door. A cold breeze swooshed through the foyer, and a few drops of rain licked at the eaves. A shadow passed by the picture window, and the door creaked. The streetlamps already glowed in the dark.

Bracken popped his head in.

"Anybody home?"

Amelia jumped up from her chair behind the desk.

"Come on in," she said. "Tori and I were just chatting, but I think we're done for now. Can I get you a cup of coffee or tea?"

He held up a hand and shook his head.

"No thanks. Tori and I are going to take a little walk. I mean, if she still wants to."

Amelia gave him a disapproving look, lips pursed and eyelids lowered.

Tori's head still spun with the horror she'd experienced in the bathroom. She still wasn't completely convinced the snakes weren't real, but perhaps the thing that scared her the most was the possibility that it *hadn't* been real. If it was all in her head, what the hell was wrong with her?

She considered canceling, but he stood there, smiling at her, and she felt the same awkward, wonderful, uncomfortable rush she'd experienced at the bar. Besides, getting outside, even in the rain, would probably be good for her. Clear her head. Get herself together.

She stood, and he put his fingertips on the small of her back as he led her out the door and into the light, cold sprinkle.

Droplets collected in her already-damp hair, and she brushed it back, pulling it to one side.

They walked down the sidewalk and crossed the empty, sand-strewn street to the splintered boardwalk. The gray clouds rose up above the swelling ocean, gray against even darker gray. It seemed appropriate.

Awnings over Victorian B&Bs along Beach Drive fluttered. The shadowy outline of a family on bikes passed them, speeding up, perhaps to escape the coming storm. Why did she agree to come out in the dark and the rain again? Had she been trying to be cute and flirty? Now, what she wanted more than anything, was to go back to her room and sleep and never dream again.

They passed the Rusty Nail and the dainty B&Bs gave way to cheaper accommodations and motels with pools and free HBO. The dead end and the gazebo appeared in the distance. They walked, stiff and silent. The world's last payphone stood, waiting for the one person in the world who didn't have a cellphone—someone who might be her.

The rain pelted down, cold and unyielding. Bracken ran ahead of her. She jerked forward and pumped her legs to keep up. Her sweater clung to her, and the pull of wet wool felt suffocating. She tugged at the neckline and readjusted her clothes. After a few seconds of inundation, she let the garments sag against her body and jogged faster.

Bracken sat on a bench under the shelter by the time she arrived and had pulled out his phone and a set of earbuds. He rearranged the cords and motioned for her to sit next to him. She pulled her dripping sweater up so that it was square on her shoulders and wrung out the excess water at the hem. Wind whipped from the ocean. The waves heaved beneath them, spraying up to the gazebo. Seawater settled against her face.

"This isn't much of a shelter, is it?" she asked.

He shrugged, and the sides of his lips curled.

"It's only water."

Her laugh, throaty and loud, caught her off-guard. She couldn't remember having had occasion to laugh about much these past several months. The vibrations behind her ribs felt good, but that sensation soon gave way to a writhing terror that wormed around in her gut. She tried to push it down and forget it.

She sat, and he offered her the right earbud, which she placed inside her ear.

The dreamy, dramatic guitar of Bryan Ferry's *Windswept* hummed in her ear. He'd been her fifth-grade crush. She'd seen the video for Roxy Music's More Than This on MTV, and thus was born her type. Tall. Dark-haired. British. More than a little smarmy and smug. Decidedly *not* the man who sat beside her sharing his music on Pandora. The brassy, sultry saxophone wailed, windswept on the air.

She saw him out of the corner of her eye. Not tall, not British, not dark-haired. Not smarmy. Not that she knew a hell of a lot about him. He may have been a nasty jerk who tortured small animals while cackling with glee. But she doubted it. And she silently wondered if that didn't fit better with the types of men she typically chose.

The song swelled along with the tide. They could've been waiting out a storm on the Mediterranean, soaked and breathless in each other's arms. Instead, she picked at a hangnail and looked out at the squall. The waves rose up and smashed against the black jetty.

The music faded out, and she felt his eyes on her. She turned to him and pulled the earbud from her ear.

"Thanks for letting me share your music. You think this is going to blow over soon?"

He smiled.

"It's the season. You never can tell. So, tell me. Why on earth don't you have a phone? I was kind of thinking back at the bar that maybe you were just trying to blow me off."

She sighed.

"Oh, boy. That's a long story that's probably going to make me sound crazy. I'll give you the short version. I got fired. I decided to come down here, maybe get some rest, a break from the hectic pace—and some other things. I turned off my phone and drove down here. I turned my phone back on and found messages from people who weren't really my friends. These folks just wanted to hear some juicy gossip they could pass on, some little tidbit about me losing my shit that could act as an icebreaker and help them land a deal or woo a client. It was just too fake."

She held out her hands and shrugged.

"So I threw my phone in the Atlantic," she said, motioning behind them.

He nodded.

"Yeah. I can understand why chucking it all in the ocean might make sense. I wish I could do that some days. Only thing is, I'm kind of connected at the hip to this thing. The bar is funny these days. We still get a flock of tourists from time to time, and I never know when I'll be asked to come in. Still, some people ..."

They both chuckled now. She felt at ease, and she opened her mouth to tell him about the strange experiences she'd been having but shut it quickly, determined not to send him bolting into the sea.

"Tell me about Chris Silver and that fight again," she said, leaning a little closer, fascinated and confounded by the tale.

"What's there to tell? He was at the Nail back in, oh, I guess it was July. Height of tourist season around here. And there's this Staten Island asshole with his wifebeater on, tattoos up and down his arms, douchebag Pauly D hairdo. And he starts wailing on his girl. Knocked one of her teeth out and put a knife under her chin. I mean, I guess Chris did what anyone would've done. He gut-punched the motherfucker, and he swiped Chris across the face with the knife."

It was so matter-of-fact, as if this sort of thing happened in the bar every day. She suspected he was being clever. Perhaps his wit was drier than she gave him credit for.

"What you're telling me is, this guy is batshit crazy?"

He nodded slowly, staring into the swirling sea.

"That would be an understatement."

He turned to face her. The sparkle of his blue eyes made her breath catch in her throat. He put a hand behind her neck and pulled her toward him. His scruffy, rough lips pressed against hers. The stubble scratched her face, just beside her lips. His tongue poked into her mouth. There was something reptilian and wrong about it. She pushed his shoulders away.

"I'm sorry, am I moving too fast? It's just that ..."

She watched a snake wiggle just above his tongue. The tubular outline inched forward, twisting back and forth seductively. A scaly belly jutted out from between his teeth and onto his mouth.

The wind swept her hair as she ran. Her shoes slapped the puddles on the boardwalk. A flagpole clanged over and over as a wrapped flag whipped around. It rang like an alarm going off in her head. Someone called over her shoulder, a desperate plea for her to slow down and come back, but it was muffled by her own heartbeat and the constant thrum of rain around her.

A block away from the Seaside, she veered off the boardwalk and down a set of steps back to the street. A car was just pulling away from a red light, but she dashed across anyway. Safely on the other side of the street, she looked over her shoulder. Bracken was nowhere to be seen. She sucked wind and pressed her hands on her knees. Her breath came in shuddering heaves, but she had to compose herself before going upstairs.

Thudding feet against the boardwalk planks made her stand upright. Bracken made his way down the steps. She ran up to Seaside House's porch. The front door was closed now, blocking out the torrential downpour.

Amelia wasn't at her desk, so she darted upstairs and sealed herself up in her bedroom.

The hem of her sweater now drooped clownishly around her thighs. Her feet squished around in her shoes, so she yanked them off and kicked them across the floor. She pulled off her sweater and slipped out of her soaked jeans. Amelia had replaced the towels in the bathroom, a small gesture for which she was eternally grateful. She wrapped her hair into a turban and clunked around in the armoire for her terrycloth robe.

She sat in her disheveled bed, wondering how she could make all of this stop. Was Amelia right? Was it a matter of just not drinking? Was this related to drinking at all? It was possible the stress had finally gotten to her and caused some sort of psychotic episode. A lot of things were possible. Speculation was not something she indulged in frequently. Her livelihood depended upon proven strategies and hard data, not Kentucky windage. She had to do *something*.

The windows were still open, and rain pattered on the sill and the hardwood floor just inside. She got up, crossed the room in a few strides, and slammed them shut hard enough to rattle the panes.

Just beyond the droplets on the glass, Bracken came into view, drenched and holding a hand over his eyes. He stood, soaked to the bone, and waved at her. The defeat in his face tugged at her, but she couldn't ignore what she'd seen. Dragging someone else through her problems, whatever they might be, seemed like the cruelest thing of all. Tori drew the feather-light curtains and walked away.

She flopped down on the bed and tried to think of other things. What she really wanted, what she really *needed*, was a drink. That desire to block all of this out, to numb it so completely that it was a black tarp over the pain, was etched on her bones. The tremor in her hands worked its way up to her shoulders and into her torso so that every part of her trembled and quaked.

Tomorrow. She decided tomorrow would be the day she'd seek out some help. Maybe she could get Amelia to help her find a meeting. If Amelia was right and these visions, these terrors, she was experiencing were down to her drinking, it was time to kick the habit for good.

She pulled her robe tight around her neck and relished the comfort. She slid beneath the sheets and listened to the rain tap the roof until her eyes drooped. She sank into the lumpy mattress, embraced by the lull of sleep.

It seemed like no time had passed at all, but sometime during the night, her eyes snapped open at the sensation she was being watched. The lamp by the bed still glowed, and she felt disoriented from waking up in a strange room with a strange light.

The curtains swayed and danced in some sort of invisible wind. The windows remained shut. The storm had abated, and only drips from the eaves and the awning remained. A face appeared from the folds and lines of the cloth. A slit of a mouth offset two evil eyes. The eyebrows were pressed together in hatred. The curve of the cheek was familiar, that of the girl in the nightmares she had so often.

She pressed her knees into her chest. The breeze picked up until she had to wrap herself in the blanket to stop the squall from freezing her through. It was as if someone cranked the air conditioner to the coldest setting and put it on full blast.

A gravelly voice echoed in her head: *Go to the phone. It's for you.*

She glanced at the antique telephone on the nightstand, but

she knew—*how did she know* —that wasn't the phone the voice meant. The shakes eased, and she threw off the blankets. The room was still frigid, and her feet seared against the wooden floor as she stood. The now-familiar stench of alcohol-tinged sweat filled her nose, and she realized it was her own. The booze seeped from her pores.

Tiny hairs stood on end at the back of her neck. She was overcome by the feeling of someone charging at her. This threatening thing propelled her out the bedroom door, down the stairs, and out into the chill of the October night. Her bare feet froze against the rain-drenched grass, but she ignored the shooting pain that went up her legs and walked, arms pumping and legs burning, across the street and down the boardwalk. The threatening presence lurked at her back. It felt so real, she looked over her shoulder, only to find the glow of streetlamps and the outline of cars parked at the meters on Beach. That reassurance did nothing to stop her feet from moving, nearly running now, splintered and bitten.

The trill of the payphone rang out as she drew closer to the dead end, a bright jingle at first. Breathless anxiety tightened her chest as she approached, and the peal turned into an angry reverberation.

She extended her hand and felt electricity course down to her elbow. The glossy black plastic felt like a chunk of ice in her fingers. Her mouth went dry, and she coughed hoarsely to catch her breath. A crackle sizzled from the earpiece. She pressed it to her ear.

How does it feel? How does it feel to be haunted every moment of the day, every second of the night? You can't just drink your problems away anymore, Victoria.

The voice dripped with contempt when it said her name. A

shock went down her spine as she listened.

You took my girl from me. She was everything in the world I had, and you ripped her out of my arms. Now she's lying in a cold box in the ground instead of smiling and laughing and going out with her friends. How does it feel to know you'll never be able to run away from that? You can't erase her with a bottle.

The phone went silent for a moment, and she pulled the phone away.

Victoria. Victoria.

The voice was insistent. It was not done with her yet.

Victoria? Victoria? Are you there? It's Mom. Honey, are you there?

"Mom? What's the matter? How can you be calling me here? You don't even know where I am."

The sound of her own high-pitched, tear-swallowed voice irritated her.

Victoria? It's your father. Oh, God, how can I even tell you this? He's dead. Honey, Dad is gone.

"Dead? How? What happened? Mom? What's wrong?"

The line went dead. The earpiece gouged into the flesh of her ear, and she listened to the drone of the dial tone until a robotic voice said, "If you'd like to make a call, please hang up and try again."

Her knees crashed onto the concrete, and a wave of tears rolled up and out of her. Every part of her, from the strands of her hair to the bottoms of her feet ached. She envisioned her father, yellow and bloated, his eyes closed in death's repose. Was it real? Was anything real? She wailed, fists scraped and bloody as she pounded them against the sidewalk, wishing it all away with every strike, hoping somehow beating the hell out of herself would make it false.

Boop-boop-beep. If you'd like to make a call, please hang up and try ...

A pair of arms hefted her up. Tori swung around, legs wobbling and unsteady, ready to use what was left of her waning strength to either fight or flee.

Amelia held up her hands. Tori fell into her warm arms and buried her head into her chest.

She pulled back a moment and wiped snot from her nose with the back of her hand.

"I want help," she whimpered. "I need help. Will you help me?"

Amelia's chest heaved in a deep breath. She closed her eyes a moment, and when she opened them again, she nodded.

"Come on. It's freezing out here. I'll start a fire."

CHAPTER 11

Amelia poked the glowing logs farther back and tossed two more onto the popping fire. It rose up, casting long shadows on the sitting room. The armchair Tori curled herself into loomed ominously in the glow.

Amelia went to the closet at the corner and rifled through some papers in a box. She retrieved a pile of pamphlets and business cards. Tori clutched her mug of tea and looked puzzled.

She shoved the pile at her, and Tori took them, glancing over the titles. Amelia knew them all by heart. "AA and You," "AA for the Woman," "Do You Think You're Different," "Inside AA," and "Is There an Alcoholic in Your Life?"

Yes. There was an alcoholic in her life, and it wasn't the first time. She'd packed all those things into the closet after Bill died, and she'd never wanted to see them again. But she couldn't turn away someone in need. She already felt like she could have done more to stop Bill from the slow suicide he chose.

Tori glanced over some of the pamphlets and sipped her drink. They might have been two old friends having a sleepover. Amelia wagered Tori's ghost stories were a lot more terrifying than any of the ones she might have to offer.

"How's your tea? Do you need more?"

Tori shook her head.

"No. Thank you."

It was the first time she'd spoken since the two trudged back into the house. She'd been in a dead sleep when she heard someone thunder down the stairs and bolt out of the front door. Chasing a lunatic down the boardwalk in the middle of the night was not how she'd planned to spend her night.

"We need to talk," Amelia said.

Tori pulled her mug away from her lips and leaned forward, knocking the pamphlets onto the floor.

"I'm sorry about …"

"No. Listen. I lied to you. I lie to everyone about it, really. People who don't know the truth anyway. My husband didn't die of cancer. He was an alcoholic. At the end of his life, he was yellow, *completely* yellow, with tubes sticking out of him. He'd always been fit, but in the final days, his belly was so bloated, he looked like a woman about to give birth. And do you know what he wanted more than anything as he lay there, struggling to breathe on his own? He wanted a fucking drink. It ate him alive. God, I know I sound preachy, and that's part of the reason I never really talk about this to anyone, because the last thing I want people to think of me is that I'm some holier-than-thou bitch. I've got my vices. Everyone does. But Jesus H. Christ, Tori, you're killing yourself."

Tori sat stunned for a moment, looking beyond Amelia. She took a long drink from her mug and looked into Amelia's eyes at last.

"I don't think there's any hope for me," she said. "This is beyond alcoholism. My ghosts have come to haunt me."

Amelia wanted to pummel her, to smack some sense into her dim head. She clenched her fists and inhaled.

"Please." She kept her voice even and detached. "Please come with me to a meeting tomorrow. We'll find the earliest one we can. Just come and see. Try. That's all I'm asking."

Tori pressed her lips into a straight line, and her eyes went to the pamphlets below.

"I'll go. I don't know if they can help me, but I'll go."

A fiery ball of light burst through the gauzy curtain. Tori snapped her head forward, still clutching a mug with the amber dregs of tea at the bottom. The sun was finally up. It felt like an eternal night, and she was grateful that the sun had bothered to rise at all. When she pulled her head off the cushion, a jolt of pain shot all the way up to her jaw. She winced and rubbed her neck, tilting her head side to side.

A tuft of dark hair peeked over the arm of the sofa on the far end of the room. Amelia snored softly.

Tori put down a foot and slid across the pamphlets. Shit. AA. She'd agreed to go to a meeting this morning, even though it felt like a waste of time. Something was after her, and even if she never touched a drop again, it would find her. Any other time, she might not have cared. She might have just let it take her. But a longing settled deep in her gut to get over this and to maybe even find happiness. Didn't she deserve to be happy? Or was that something reserved only for people who'd never killed anyone? Karma balanced things out. She'd taken a life, and, in turn, her life had crumbled around her. Only karma wasn't enough. Whatever chased her, it was out for blood.

The memory of that phone call buzzed in her head. Amelia bore witness to the fact that she'd actually left the house. That much really happened, she decided. Piecing the rest together might prove tricky.

She'd wait until Amelia was up and ask if she could call her mother. That would settle the biggest worry weighing on her this morning. If her father was dead or alive, there was little she could do about it. She didn't want to alarm her mother though. She hadn't called home in years, not after Dad called her a self-centered bitch during one of his benders. The words still stung. Dad was the King of the Self-Centered Bitches, a man so determined to destroy his life that he was more than happy to take down everyone around him, too. Mom, for reasons she couldn't fathom, stuck by his side and had effectively disowned her. It wasn't a conversation she was eager to have, but it was one she *needed* to have.

Amelia groaned and rolled over.

"What time is it?" she asked.

"Seven thirty-five," Tori said, glancing at the grandfather clock by the fireplace.

"Ugh. Okay, I'm up."

She turned herself upright and put a hand to her forehead.

"We can probably find a meeting soon. Let me grab my phone, and I'll let you know what I find."

One eye still closed, her hair gathered up on her head like a nest, she made her way down the hall to the office. Tori followed at a distance and said, "Hey, do you mind if I use your phone to call home? I'm still pretty upset about last night. I'll pay you back if there are any extra charges."

A little *pppfffttt* sound puffed from her lips.

"Unlimited minutes. You're good. Let me just look up an AA

meeting around here, and we'll go. After breakfast, though. I'm starving."

The glow from the phone lit up Amelia's face, and for the first time, Tori noticed the woman's true beauty. Her eyes were almond-shaped, suggesting some Asian ancestry. She had a small, flat nose and cherubic lips that pouted slightly as she scrolled through her options on the phone. Something shined beyond her smooth skin, deep within. There was a tenderness to her eyes, like a child in a Millais painting.

"Ah," she said, straightening herself. "Here we go. Looks like the Rio Grande Universalist Fellowship has a meeting at 10. We have plenty of time to grab a bite."

She handed over her phone.

"Go ahead and make your call. I'm gonna run upstairs and make myself look human again."

The slim phone felt heavy in her hand. She knew the old landline number by heart; it was the same one she'd had as a kid, but the thought of punching in the numbers made her throat go dry. She could even imagine the light beige AT&T telephone in the rec room *brrrriiinnngg*-ing, and her mother picking up on the first ring. There was no answering machine. Dad never figured out how to set them up, and both her parents figured if they'd gone through life without leaving messages or having messages left for them, they could still survive without the technology.

Tori was halfway up the steps, the phone still in her palm, when she brushed up against a section of yellow floral wallpaper that flapped up. She put a hand to it and held it in place, hoping to smooth it out and affix it to the wall, but it had long lost its bond.

Something moved beneath the paper surface. Tori could only watch as a large lump moved its way across the tattered wallpaper. An illusion, she decided. It had to have been something in the print or a trick of the light.

It was enough to send her charging up the stairs and into her suite. The moment she closed the bedroom door, a cheerful tune jingled on the cellphone in her hand. She looked at the screen. UNKNOWN CALLER. The little ditty ... *was it playing louder now?* ... continued to chime. *Shouldn't the voicemail have picked up by now?* She pressed the Talk button and put the phone to her ear.

"Hello?"

The word came out cracked and dusty.

Static crackled on the other end. A sound like metal swirling against metal followed, as if a ladle rubbed against the bottom of a copper pot.

"Dad ... Daddy ... Dah ...'s day. Daid. Dayed."

The static hissed and popped. A New England accent, no-nonsense but polite, struggled against it, and Tori could only pick up sounds and parts of words.

"Hello? Hello? Who's there? I can't understand you," Tori said.

A flush of heat overcame her, and she wanted to hit the End button. A crossed wire, a wrong number, a stupid prank. All she had to do was hit the End button.

Still, she wanted to know.

A demonic, hacking laugh broke through on the line. The voice taunted, "Daddy's dead. Daddy's dead. Daddy's dead. And you're gonna die next."

The phone zapped her hand, and she dropped it to the floor with a *thud*. She put a hand to her mouth.

"Everything okay? Are you ready to go?" Amelia called from the bottom of the staircase. "I don't know about you, but I'm starving."

The last thing she wanted to do was eat. Her body quaked as she moved to the desk and grabbed the airplane bottle of Fireball, unscrewed the cap, and tipped it back. The cinnamon shot burned down her throat, but the taste hardly mattered. It was medicine. It might as well have been Dimetapp or Theraflu. Shudders rippled from her chest to her limbs. A shot usually eased the shakes in a matter of seconds. That warm radiation was oddly absent this time. Cold tremors ached her bones. She unsnapped the cap from the gin and chugged it until the fumes tingled her nose hairs, and she felt breathless. The bottle *chunked* against the wood as she set it back down, and she gasped for air.

"You okay?" Amelia hollered up.

Footsteps clonked up the stairs, and she knew she'd have to fix herself up. Amelia was ready to kick her ass to the curb.

She tucked the empty bottle into a trash can, pulled a wad of Kleenexes from the box on the desk, and covered it up. Then she tiptoed to the bathroom.

"I'll only be a minute," she said. "Just need to get dressed."

At the vanity, she saw a haggard, puffed mess. Dark, swollen rings encircled her eyes. Her hair frizzed in all directions. It could've been the bad lighting, but her skin looked sallow.

She ran a comb over her hair and pulled it into a loose ponytail. She scooped some cold tap water into her palms and splashed it against her face. It smelled like rust, but it made her eyes feel less like boiled eggs.

She went to the armoire, pulled out a hoodie, and sifted through the pile of clothes on the floor for a pair of jeans. A white piece of paper stuck up from the back pocket of the jeans. It was the card from that guy at the Rusty Nail. Chris. Chris Silver, the delusional man who wanted to save her. She laughed at the idea that someone *could* save her as she pulled them over her hips. She studied the card and stuffed it back into her pocket.

The liquor bottles taunted her on the other side of the armoire, and she stared longingly back at the gin. Would it be so horrible to take a little more, just to take the edge off? Would Amelia smell it on her and kick her out? What sort of fucked-up, matronly hold on her did Amelia have anyway? There were other places in Cape May. Still, there was something about Amelia that made her want the woman's approval. She didn't have a lot of friends—not real ones anyway, and Amelia was a kind person who'd shown her compassion. Plus, she'd lost her husband to drinking, something that scared Tori more than a little. It seemed like a hokey, Hallmark card sentiment, but she wanted to stop drinking to make Amelia proud of her.

As if on cue, Amelia knocked at the door. Tori tucked her feet into a fresh pair of wool socks and pulled on her still-wet sneakers.

"All set," she said through the door and opened it.

She'd never been more eager to leave a place in her life.

Outside, a chill hovered in the air in the wake of the storm. The sun edged its way over the ocean, but it offered little in the way of warmth. Tori pulled her hoodie up over her head and shoved her frozen fingers into her pockets.

It was a quiet trek along the sidewalk. A couple walked their German shepherd. They nodded a greeting. A sandpiper hopped from morsel to morsel strewn along Beach Drive. Her stomach gurgled as they walked. They passed hokey palm trees that looked strange here. But, then again, so did the tacky mint-green colored motels they grew near. The east side of the island looked dignified, with its brightly colored mansions staring out at the sea like painted-up war widows waiting for their fighting men to come home. It was a place for well-to-do New Yorkers on holiday from the city heat and grime. The west side looked like 1954 threw up and the mess was never mopped up. It was a bizarre collision of eras, but Tori liked this side. Childhood summers were spent getting tossed into the pool by her shitfaced Pop. Tacky, threadbare carpeting and smelly, polyester comforters were a constant in those memories. This side of the cape seemed less judgmental. The snobby lifestyle she'd lived back in Montclair didn't fit her. She'd *wanted* it to. She'd been led to believe, maybe by the men in her life, that was the thing to strive for. A cold, sterile apartment with cold, sterile friends. Cocktails at the bar and trips to Paris or London every summer. That façade itched. It was too tight across the chest.

She was just some New England girl whose father drank too much PBR and Jameson and whose mother dutifully mopped up the mess and tucked old Dad into bed to sleep it off until the next time.

Amelia led her to a small café on a side street situated across from a towering oak. Tori smashed her toes against a jumbled, cracked segment of sidewalk pushed up by the oak's roots and nearly toppled forward.

"That's about all the excitement I'm prepared for this morning," she said, trying to save face.

Amelia pressed her lips together and gave her a side-eyed glance.

The hostess at the Buttered Biscuit led them to a light-drenched table with a street view. Tourists flitted about, more than she would've imagined on a chilly day.

Amelia propped her elbows on the table and rested her chin on her intertwined fingers.

"You were drinking earlier, weren't you?"

Cold prickled at Tori's neck.

"No. Of course not."

Amelia sneered.

"I'm not stupid. I can smell it on you."

She leaned in and lowered her voice.

"You're not dealing with an amateur here. My husband drank every single day. Couldn't function without the stuff."

She paused a moment, and her features softened.

"I'm not a bitch. I get that you're struggling. That's why I want to help. God knows, maybe I could've done more to help Bill. Maybe this is my second chance to help someone who's drowning. I don't know. I was raised in a Catholic household, and I was always taught that people come into our lives for a reason. Whether or not you accept my help is up to you, of course, but do not mistake my kindness for weakness. My help comes with an expiration date."

She leaned back in her chair and looked at the menu as if they'd been discussing the unpredictable weather and it was time to move to another subject.

"I feel like pancakes today. How 'bout you? Anything look good?"

Tori sat there for a moment, drinking in the lecture she'd just received. She didn't want pancakes or anything else for that matter, but she scanned the menu and considered her options.

Something horrible flashed in her head. It flickered like a grainy 70s exploitation film in her mind. Red splattered her clothes, and she clutched a knife in her white, knobby knuckles. She brought it down again and again into Amelia's chest, pulling up viscera and blood as she swung it back down again.

The vision made her gasp and put a hand to her face. Amelia glanced up from her menu and said, "Everything all right? I hear they make really great omelets. Never tried one myself."

Tori's mouth hung open for a moment. That flash of remorseless violence was not something she'd even consider, let alone try to enact. She pushed the thought from her mind and said, "Yeah, maybe I'll try an omelet. Haven't had one in a while."

Food might do her some good. She hadn't eaten much over the past couple of days, and her jeans already gapped at the back.

The waitress took their order, and they sat in uncomfortable silence, watching people go into the few shops and restaurants that were open after Labor Day. Amelia pulled her phone from her pocket and scanned it.

"Hm. Did someone call when you were upstairs?" she asked.

Tori's mouth went dry.

"Yeah. The phone rang, but it was an unknown caller. Probably a wrong number."

If she'd told her the truth, she'd just chalk it up to a drunken hallucination. But there was proof after all that maybe something dreadful *had* called her on Amelia's phone, something determined to reach her at any cost.

CHAPTER 12

The Rio Grande Unitarian Universalist Fellowship's basement looked like a 1970s rec room with its wood paneling, green shag carpeting, and a foosball table positioned along the far wall. It smelled like four decades worth of casseroles.

Metal folding chairs filled the center of the space, and a bespectacled guy in a green sweater vest stood at a lectern at the front.

Amelia stepped into the room and asked, louder than Tori wanted, "Is this the AA meeting?"

The man nodded once, and she and Tori took seats near the back.

"We're waiting on a few regulars," the man said. "We'll get started in just a minute."

The door clanged shut behind them, and Tori turned to see Bracken the Bartender walk in. What kind of shit was this? He served alcohol for a living, and he was in AA? She was so puzzled, she almost walked up to him, but the fear of what she'd seen at the gazebo, the fear of everything that had been happening to her recently, glued her to her spot.

He looked fresh and rugged in the mid-morning sunlight streaming through the basement windows. For a moment, she forgot about her troubles, and something she hadn't felt in a long time stirred within her—the desire to love and be loved. He held the door for a few seconds, and a dark-haired woman wearing large sunglasses walked in behind him and took his hand. All of the air in Tori's body streamed out. Wife? Girlfriend? Maybe she was a sister. She didn't look old enough to be his mother.

He led her by the hand to a seat near the front and turned to face Tori before they sat. He didn't seem flustered at all by her presence there. He didn't turn around again.

The door opened again, and two more people entered, a short, balding man in a flannel shirt and trucker's cap and a middle-aged woman in a sweater dress.

The man in the vest said, "I think we're just about ready. Anyone want to start?"

The woman at the front with Bracken stood up and said, "My name is Andrea, and I'm an alcoholic. It's been seventy-six days since my last drink."

She droned like a Catholic confessing her sins. The whole thing seemed mighty judgmental for a Unitarian church, and Tori felt the sting of embarrassment upon her cheeks at the memory of Bracken's burning lips upon hers. She'd have to stand up in front of everyone, including him, and admit she had a problem she wasn't sure she was ready to admit she had.

She listened intently to Andrea talk about how last week was a struggle, especially since Bracken won't stop drinking himself.

"Well, part of recovery is living in a world where people drink," the man at the lectern said. "Don't be too critical of your husband."

Husband. *Husband!*

Tori leapt up and banged into the chair next to her. Amelia's fingers dug into her arm, but she jerked away and sprang out the door, which slammed with a *chunk*. The metal clunk of the door rang out again, but she was halfway up the stairs. She was about to shove open the front door when Amelia wheeled her around and said, "What the fuck is going on with you? You're here to get help?"

"I thought you weren't going to nag me about this anymore," Tori spat.

Amelia reached around her and pressed a hand against the door, shutting her in. Tori tried to pull the door open, but the slight woman was stronger than she looked.

"I think you need to get your things out of my house and leave. I've told you the conditions for living in my home. And if you're unwilling to cooperate, you must go. I'll escort you back to the house, and you get your things. If you refuse, I'll just call the police."

Heat rose from within her clothes. It came with a bizarre nausea that almost made her puke. She doubled over for a moment, effectively homeless. Could she go back there and watch Bracken, Bracken who had pressed his bloodless lips against hers, help his alcoholic wife? She lurched forward and out the door.

Anxiety sank its claws into her chest for the whole walk back to Seaside House. Her breath came in gasps. Amelia wouldn't even look at her. She walked, back stick-straight, like a marching robot. They climbed the front steps.

"Look, I'm sorry. I want to go back. I can stop. I promise. I won't touch another drop."

Amelia stared blankly ahead and pointed to the stairwell leading to the honeymoon suite.

Tori walked up a few steps and stopped. The peeling yellow wallpaper rippled on a breeze. Something froze her to the spot, the sensation of something worming its way through her bloodstream. It wasn't warm and radiant like the first gulps of liquor. It was cold and scaly. It had fangs.

This bitch has to die. The blurry, delirious thing that lived in her blood whispered it in her ear. Her movements were controlled by this serpentine phantom. She climbed again, Amelia at her back. Tori hesitated at the door, paralyzed by what she had to do on the other side. The thing that had overtaken her was black and sticky and feasted upon the blood of others. Tori wanted to run to the ocean and drown herself there, swallow all the saltwater on the planet and sink to the bottom where the fish could eat her eyes. But this thing, it held her steady at the door, it turned the knob, it sent her directly to the table with the bottles. Amelia crossed her arms over her chest and watched, mouth turned downward in its judgmental disapproval.

Who asked this bitch for her opinion, it growled in her head.

Tori's hand clutched the glass gin bottle. Queen Victoria scowled from the label. It felt simultaneously weightless and heavy. Tori held it up by the neck. Anger sizzled her scalp. *Can I stop myself now?* she wondered. *Could I take another path?* But her muscles moved. Something fluttered in front of her. A butterfly flapped its wings furiously, as if waving her off, pleading with her to fight it and regain control of her life. Her arm propelled itself forward and the bottle made a sickly *blonk* as it smashed into the flesh of Amelia's head. She expected—*wanted?*—a scream, but Amelia only raised her hands and batted at the glass as it thudded against her forehead. Spatter ricocheted in slow motion and settled on Tori's face and hands. The butterfly crumpled, imprinted in red, against the mass of viscera. The tiny black legs twitched. The wings trembled. Soon, it was still, smeared in goop. Deep red flowed from a spot beneath her clotted hair. Amelia went to her knees at first, putting her fingers to her scalp and pulling them away to see the damage inflicted. She flopped forward, thudding her chin against the hardwood floor. Tori brought the bottle down again, and it struck the back of her head with a cartoonish *clunk*. The sparks of life waned and died out.

The bottled slipped from Tori's hand. She stared at the woman sprawled face down. Dread prickled up her arms. Her chest huffed in jagged bursts, and small animal whines worked up from her guts. Her insides twisted, and she fell to the floor next to Amelia and tried to pick her up. She hooked her forearms under the woman's limp armpits and pulled up. She was dead weight. Amelia's mouth fell open and her tongue edged its way out.

Tori brought the body back down across her lap and smacked the bloody face with her palm, willing her to wake up and move. Amelia's skin felt wet and cold. Soon, the soggy sound of skin slapping skin made Tori recoil, and she shoved Amelia's body away from her.

Tori scampered backward until she slumped against the wood of the bed. She climbed over the footboard and scurried to the headboard. She stuffed a pillow into her face and screamed.

When all the air had been expended from her lungs, she shoved herself under the fluff of the blankets and rocked back and forth. The only light that came into the comforter-cocoon was the dull lamplight that peeked through the borders. Her breath was irregular and before long, the black sucked her in completely.

The bombastic crash of a headache wrenched Tori from the blackout. Her knuckles ached as she clutched the thick blanket against her face. She released the cloth and pulled it back, body trembling at the thought of what might greet her on the other side. Silence. Beyond the windows, the ocean breathed in and out. A light breeze flapped the purple awning that covered the deck just below her room. It seemed ... *normal*. How could anything be normal?

Her body swayed upright. Sunlight, soft and serene, filtered through the thin curtains. She threw her legs over the edge of the bed and flung herself to the floor. She crawled on her hands and knees across the hardwood around the bed.

She held her breath and closed her eyes. She opened them, expecting to see a tangled mass of black-blood and goop tangled in Amelia's hair, her body cold and blue against the floor, puddles spreading out across the otherwise polished floorboards.

Instead, she saw nothing. The floor was clean and bare where Amelia should've been. The gin bottle was clean and bright on the writing desk where it tempted her with its bittersweet promise of relief. She heeded its call and pushed herself to her feet. Tori inspected the bottle for some sign, *any* sign, that it had been used as a weapon. She stared at the clean, clear glass for cracks or blood droplets. When she found nothing, she twisted the cap and swigged it. The medicinal fluid flooded her mouth and quenched the undying urge that itched beneath her flesh.

The buzz coursed through her veins, but the sledgehammer headache hit her so hard, she nearly collapsed. She had to know, so she turned and made her way, step by excruciating step, to the stairwell. Tori clutched the dark oak railing and made her way down. The trip took much longer than it should have. If her body still belonged to her, she would've thrown herself down from the top floor. But she couldn't even force herself to do that. It wanted her to suffer.

On the bottom landing, she steadied herself against the wall. The flap of yellow wallpaper scratched her leg. Her ears strained. The silence saturated the room so thick, it overwhelmed her and made her dizzy. The room blurred. She took a tentative step off the landing and onto the threadbare rug that ran the expanse of the foyer. The desk was cluttered with papers. The back edge of the desk was lined with photographs in silver, contemporary frames. It looked out of place in a house decorated top to bottom in Victoriana. All of the photos were of Amelia and her husband. He'd been handsome. A beard that could've used a trim exploded from his face, but a pair of expressive eyes peeked out from the hair. He looked strong and fit, almost like a Viking. He seemed an odd match for someone as unassuming as Amelia. Still, their faces beamed in the photographs. He held her from behind, resting his head on her shoulder in one. In another, he knelt on one knee, arm outstretched to her, as if he was serenading her in silent song. Her face was permanently frozen in love glow, eyes aflutter to the sky, hand on heart. A moment in twilight. Sun through the window illuminated a million dust motes. Tori's guts turned and tears gurgled up and burned her sinuses. She tried to call out, but her voice hitched in her throat.

It was all overwhelming, and desperation flickered for just a moment in her mind. That desire for an easy way out sparked back to life. There was a time, maybe hundreds of crises ago, when she would've chosen the door out. Pills or a rope over the shower rod. She'd pulled herself out of enough jams to know she'd done it before, and it could be done again. She just had to figure out what was going on. That seemed like an insurmountable task now, but she'd puzzle it out.

She'd been broke, living off of canned tuna and stale, outlet store bread after Tim kicked her out. There were days the vacant, growling hunger and emotional despair of being disposed of like a holey pair of socks nearly knocked her out of the game. But she'd held fast. She pulled together a hodgepodge of clients, one more ragtag than the last. These companies were mostly on the brink of bankruptcy and could only afford barebones marketing campaigns. Some of them survived thanks to her services. Some failed. But she thrived. Soon, those companies that benefited from her pluckiness started giving her referrals. And word-of-mouth got around until she moved out of the hotbox apartment into a gated community.

And just like that, she'd descended back into Hell.

Tori sucked in a breath and released it. She tried it a few more times, pressed her hands against her knees, and stepped on the balls of her feet to the back of the house.

The cherry dining room table just off the foyer was set for breakfast with gleaming china and polished silverware. She turned and walked into the kitchen. The sink was empty. Rows of glasses shone brilliantly against the sunlight coming in across the house. The tile floor was spotless. Spotless. Spots. Spots of blood everywhere. Tori clutched the edge of the granite countertop and slipped until she fell flat to the ground. Her cheek ached from the impact. The drive to *know* propelled her up off the floor and onto her feet again. There was a small bathroom off of the kitchen, and she ducked inside. Empty. She knew it would be empty. The desperation to find her propelled Tori back into the kitchen. She sucked in a long breath and retraced her steps through the still, empty house.

Back up the stairs, she stopped on the second floor. The door to Amelia's room was open, but she stalled there. Some frayed thread of decorum glued her to the spot. She couldn't invade that sanctuary, desperate as she was to know. The bed was made.

"Amelia?"

The words were hoarse and dry in her throat. The sound of her own voice in the dead silence made her stomach flop.

Silence crept around her and nearly suffocated her like a blanket.

Tori tapped on the door as if she needed something but didn't want to make too much of a fuss. *Yes, I may have just killed you, and I hope it's not too much of an imposition, but could you just show up, alive or dead, and let me know. Thanks so much!*

"Amelia?"

She listened beyond the doorway but heard nothing.

Shadows crept across the walls as the sun made its slow ascent, and she wheeled around, expecting to see *something*.

"Amelia!"

Her voice strained.

A million thoughts swirled in her mind. Had she called 911? Maybe she'd fled to seek medical attention. Tori couldn't be entirely sure she'd even hit her. A sickly green feeling wriggled up in her stomach, and she retched yellow gunk all over the floor.

None of this made sense. There had been a voice, something that compelled her to attack. Even at her drunkest, even at her angriest, she'd never so much as slapped another person. Visions of the night *that woman* attacked her at the Carriage House came flooding back. That woman was going to hit her, and all Tori could do was watch and flinch. Even then, she hadn't been able to fight back. She reasoned it all in her head, as if trying to convince a jury of spirits that settled around her in judgment.

She tiptoed around the vomit dotting the floor. Her heart caught in her throat as she pressed herself against the wall. Her ears strained for the voices, but there was nothing. She doubled over and lunged into the bathroom.

The second-floor communal bath's floor had a permanent layer of grit from thousands of sandy bare feet padding to and from the toilet and bathtub. Tori leaned over the toilet and vomited clear fluid into it. Shuddering, she peeled off her clothes and shuffled to the glass-encased shower. The mirror over the sink revealed brown-red droplets across her ghost-pale face. She screeched open the glass. Nightmare memories of the telephone booth at the dead end swirled in her mind. The voice from the phone echoed.

She stepped in and yanked the door shut until it sealed.

The water sprayed down cold at first. It shocked her back to life and gradually warmed. Red gathered at the drain, and she stumbled backward. It smelled rusty, and soon it ran clear. Tori unwrapped a bar of soap and ran it over her body, lathering up the grime and sweat that lived on her skin.

There was something about the boxed-in shower that made her feel safe and protected, even from the undulating tremors that constantly tormented her. It was the same comfort a blanket gave her. She knew the enclosure couldn't protect her, but it bought her a moment of peace, and she relished it even if she knew she'd have to leave the sanctuary and face reality sooner or later. Perhaps it was the same false sense of security that makes people hide under the blankets when they hear a strange noise in the night. Do they really think the blanket will stop someone from murdering them? Probably not. But it's soothing all the same.

She closed her eyes, letting the warmth envelope her and the soap wash away all the bad things. Her eyes snapped open at a sound she couldn't quite place. A beige outline blurred against the pebbled glass of the shower doors. Her eyes were trained on it, hunting for movement. It was statue-still. A flinch shuffled the watercolor-painting blur, and Tori gasped.

"Who's there?"

Her voice bounded off the glass. Every nerve tensed in her body. Exposed and vulnerable, a real person was far more of a threat than any ghostly figure. The enclosed shower grew darker. The chunky, grunting sound of someone clearing their throat rang out.

She pressed her back against the smooth, cold tile. A sliver of shock went down her spine. The blurred, beige blob on the other side of the glass neared. It touched the handle to the door, and the entire glass rattled.

Tori tried to breathe around the lump in her throat. Hot tears worked up in her eyes. The water continued its steady strum, but all the comfort it previously held was gone.

"Who. Is. There!"

The door edged open, and some of the shower spray trickled onto the floor.

Tori shouted. Her arms went defensively to her breasts, and her leg lifted instinctively to accommodate some modicum of modesty.

It was coming in. A yellow, puffy hand waved, almost like a party clown waves at a little kid. Its breath was heavy, perfumed with rot and the all-too-familiar fumes of booze.

"Hey, Pumpkin!"

The voice growled, hard from a life of whiskey sours and too many Marlboro Reds.

Her tears came in jagged bursts now as she watched her father climb into the shower with her. He was swollen to twice his normal size. His skin looked like a bruised banana peel.

"What's the matter, kiddo? Why don't you get on out of the shower, and I'll take you down to the Nut House for some pecan bars. Then maybe we'll hit the beach. Gotta pick up provisions first. All out of Bacardi. Whaddya say? I'll even give you a sip of my rum and Coke. It's been a while since you last had a drink. Isn't it about time for another?"

Tori stared. The water arced around him, never touching his clothes. He wore a brown sheepskin car coat and the floppy, green fisherman's hat that made him look moronic. But the hateful glare in his eyes chilled her down to her bones, and she screamed so loud, the reverberation rang out in her ears. She retreated to the tile wall behind her and raised an arm across her breasts.

"Dad?" The word croaked from her throat. The sound even shocked her.

He extended a cartoonish, bloated hand. His expression was tender and empathetic. Fatherly. The word infuriated Tori. Her father had never been fatherly.

"Come on. Get out of the shower. It's time to get something to drink. I know you're thirsty, baby."

The whole-body tremors overtook her. She needed to get out. She needed to drink. Her throat felt like hot sand. A heavy weight settled on her as she gathered her wits. If he was standing before her, bloated and smelly, a vague betrayal of himself, he must be ...

She bashed herself against the glass, and the door shimmied open. She felt exposed and scampered to pull a towel from the shelf above the toilet tank and wrapped her body in it, eyes trained on the shower.

The tinkle of water against the bare tile floor was the only sound. She couldn't see inside. The door she'd opened swayed almost shut again. She hesitated for a moment, then moved, each step a shamble. She put a hand to the door and nudged it open with her fingertips, too afraid to reach out completely, lest something clutch her by the wrist.

The stall was empty.

She stood shivering and wet, confounded and horrified.

So, the phone call was true. And it made no sense that it could be true. Had she spoken to her mother? It seemed nearly impossible that her mother would've been able to reach her on some rusted-out, sand-strewn payphone hundreds of miles from her home in New Hampshire.

She snapped out of her stupor and realized she was making crazy-assed theories about her father's death based upon a vision that might not have even been real. She shut off the faucet.

She dried herself, but the thought of going back to her room made her shudder. She'd have to face reality sooner or later, even if that reality meant jail time for walloping Amelia over the head, but now she was naked and growing colder by the minute.

Tori walked upstairs and grabbed the same gin bottle she swore she'd hit Amelia with and took a drink.

CHAPTER 13

Chris looked out over the crowd. It had been a good day. He'd sold all of the rarities he'd brought with him, plus some of the most recent issues of *Thor, Old Man Logan, American Gods, Monstress,* and *Dark Nights: Metal*. A mom came in and snapped up all of the *Wings of Fire* graphic novels for her kid, who offered Chris a lecture on why the ice dragon was the coolest one of all without the slightest hint of irony in his voice. Chris chuckled thinking about the kid. The collectible figures did well, too.

He couldn't shake the guilt of hitting that jerk the night before. Oh, there was no doubt the asshole deserved it—and worse. But, boy, did Chris feel it today. His knuckles throbbed, and there was a persistent, angry ache in his thigh. His back creaked when he stood.

Doug charged through the crowd, jolting around people and clearing a path toward him. The sight startled Chris.

"Man, you gotta pack up and get out of here," Doug blurted breathlessly.

Chris furrowed his brow. "What on earth is going on?"

"Security's looking for you. I heard them talking to some kid in the hallway. He described you to a tee and gave them the name from your nametag. Dude! The guy said you beat the shit out of him last night. What the fuck?"

Nausea washed over Chris.

"I can explain," he said, aghast at the look on Doug's face. "This kid was being very aggressive to a young woman, and he looked like he was going to get physical, so I ..."

He stopped short of telling Doug that he transformed into QuickSilver, and that the transformation is involuntary and so seamless, most people wouldn't be able to discern it. He couldn't control it any more than he could control breathing.

"I just had to. I had to step in."

Doug pressed his lips together and nodded. "I get it. Hey, I would've done the same thing. But, listen, this is serious. I think the fucker is going to press charges. I'm just giving you a heads up. You might want to start packing your shit. Here, I'll give you a hand."

The cold reality that he could go to jail settled over Chris. Doug had already started grabbing comics and putting them into boxes.

"Hey, careful with those. Here, these go in this box."

The two sorted through the merchandise on the table and loaded up the boxes onto the dolly in the corner. They made a few back-and-forth trips to Chris's car and loaded it up. Once the table was cleared, Doug stood, hands open, and said, "Nothing but respect, man, but you need some help."

Help? Chris knew what he was getting at.

"I'm not crazy," Chris asserted as they walked out of the dealers' room to the bank of elevators so he could retrieve his overnight bag.

Doug put his hands down and shook his head.

"You can't do stuff like that, man. You're gonna end up in jail. If this asshole chooses to push things, he could probably get your address from the hotel and track you down. Get on out of here, and, if you're lucky, he might drop it. If you need a witness, I'm here for you."

Doug tucked a hand into his back pocket and retrieved a business card.

"If shit gets real, give me a call."

Chris took it and nodded. He appreciated the gesture, but the last thing QuickSilver needed was a sidekick. The elevator dinged, and he extended a hand and shook Doug's. Doug pulled him in for an embrace.

"It's been so good to see you," Doug said. "I'm serious about getting together soon. Let's make a plan. You call me, y'hear?"

Chris smiled and said, "Yeah. Of course."

He genuinely liked Doug, and he appreciated that he might be a witness if anything did come of last night's fight. Being a superhero made it hard to form real friendships, and he knew their plans to meet up would probably go unfulfilled.

He made it to his room and threw a few clothing items from the night before into the overnight bag. He gave the place a once-over to make sure he hadn't forgotten anything and hauled ass to the lobby where he hastily handed his key over to Jessica, who looked frazzled and overwhelmed. She gave a weak smile as she handed over his receipt.

"Hope you had a pleasant stay," she said before turning back to her computer.

He hefted his bag to the car and headed off for the highway, checking his rearview on the way out.

Bracken watched Andrea sip a cup of tea and read her Facebook newsfeed. Her thumb flipped against the screen every few seconds. She never looked up to catch his gaze, and it made him sad.

Tori had seen him. And she'd heard. A nervous knot built in his stomach. He'd never meant for anything to happen. He loved his wife. Still, some fucked-up white knight syndrome wormed its way through his veins. It was the same compulsion that drove him to move all the way across the country to save his online girlfriend/now wife's home from foreclosure. It was the same compulsion that compelled him to plead and beg her to get help for her drinking problem. He wouldn't even drink at home. Maybe he saw parallels between the two women, but he knew Tori's problem was far worse than he could handle. Andrea'd had a binge-drinking problem. Tori might just be losing her grip on reality. He couldn't be sure just *what* had been going through her head the other night. He just couldn't stand to see a woman suffer.

He'd kissed her under the gazebo after neglecting to tell her he had a wife. And now she knew. An overwhelming urge to explain and fix things seized him. He stood up, and for the first time all morning, Andrea looked up.

"Hey, what's wrong?" she asked.

"I ... I have something I need to do. I'll be back in a little while."

He stuffed his keys in the pocket of his jeans, put on his sneakers, and opened the porch door. He felt Andrea's eyes on his back as he walked out.

Bracken put a hand to his eyes to block the sunlight. It was bright but not warm, and he wished he'd brought a flannel shirt or the cardigan that dangled by a thick cable of wool from the coatrack.

The southbound trip along a cracked and root-jumbled

sidewalk took much longer than usual. Maybe it just seemed that way. Something hung in the air. It was thick and menacing. It threatened to eclipse the sun itself and cast the trees, the Victorian homes lining Perry Street, the beach, and even his soul into darkness. He couldn't see it, but electricity sizzled down his spine, and the feathery brown hair on his arms stood on end.

The house near the intersection of Beach loomed taller than he remembered.

I'm being ridiculous, he thought. *I'm just nervous. This is awkward. Beyond awkward.*

He sucked in the briny sea air and clomped up the front steps. The front door was unlocked, so he walked on in.

Amelia wasn't at her post at the front desk.

"Amelia? Hello?"

Silence hung heavy in the air. His footsteps echoed as he moved up the stairs. A piece of wallpaper unfurled from the wall, and the rustle it made sent a jolt through his belly. His elbows snapped out in preparation for a fight. He almost laughed at himself when he realized it was only the wallpaper. Man, Amelia had really let this place go since Bill died.

It had never been the nicest place on Beach. They allowed dogs, and the whole place smelled like soggy canines and mildew from the water stains they just couldn't pull from the carpets. It was a popular choice for college kids who were happy to share a hall bathroom with ten strangers. The price reflected that. It may not have been nice, but it certainly was cheap.

It seemed those tight margins were so paper-thin, Amelia couldn't pay for repairs. He flipped the wallpaper back up and continued up to the second floor. A thud from above cracked the silence. It anchored him to the second-floor landing. His ears perked as he sought out a source for the sound. A door slammed open. Feet pounded against the wooden steps.

The rustle of cloth became more distinct as someone rounded the banister.

Tori stomped down the last few steps, wrapped in a down blanket, hair frizzed in all directions, face drawn and concrete white. Alcohol fumes wavered off of her.

A growl rumbled from deep within her. Bracken clutched the banister.

"Tori? Are you okay?"

Her gaze was intense, like a sniper coolly watching a target, determining how much time she'd need to squeeze the trigger and blast his guts all over the floor. Her pupils blacked out most of her irises. She took a few steps forward and her lips curled at the corners.

"Oh, hey."

Her hollow eyes flickered. A rosy glow spread across her cheeks. She looked *almost* normal.

"Didn't hear you come in. I'm guessing we have a lot to talk about, huh? Like the fact that you invited me out and kissed me and left out some important information?"

Bracken considered bolting for the front door, but he knew this had to be done.

"Come downstairs. Let's sit down, and I can explain."

A faint, humorless smile stretched broadly across her face. Her eyes were wild and angry.

He started down the stairs first, and he heard the bedlinens draped around Tori scratch against the wallpaper. It hissed all the way down the stairwell. A cold sweat gathered at the base of his neck. Tori's presence behind him felt ominous. He half expected to turn around and find Count Orlok hunched and claws raised, ready to draw blood.

Bracken led her to the front parlor to the left of the front door. They sat on an overstuffed sofa. Tori's blankets took up about a third of the cushion.

"Hey, listen. I just wanted to say I'm really sorry you found out I'm married the way you did. I should've been a hundred-percent honest from the get-go. There was something about you. I felt I needed to reach out to you. I've been married for fifteen years, and this is the first time, I swear, the first time I've ever done anything like this."

Bracken paused a moment, gauging her reaction, studying her face for some sign of grace or forgiveness or anger.

Tori sat stiffly, a hand clenched against the cloth of the comforter. Her eyes were focused on the picture window. He wasn't sure she'd even heard him.

"Tori? Are you okay? Do you need help?"

She turned her head slowly until her ink-black eyes connected with his. She stared, boring into his soul for a few moments. Then she leaned forward and a bony, veiny hand poked through from the comforter. She clutched his knee bone until pain shot down his thigh. He jumped up and backed to the door. Her other hand produced a bottle of clear liquor from beneath the comforter. She uncorked it and suckled deeply. When she came up for air, she laughed.

"Help? Do I need help?" she asked. Her voice was metallic and hoarse.

Her gaze went beyond the picture window to the shore.

"There's no help for me."

Bracken rubbed his knee and hobbled to the front porch. Then he shambled all the way back home, eyes scanning from time to time to make sure he wasn't being followed.

CHAPTER 14

Bilious fluid gurgled in Tori's throat. She tried to open her eyelids, but they were so heavy, the simple act seemed impossible. The floor was cold. She still clutched the empty bottle in her right hand.

A shadow crossed her face. The pressure of someone standing over her made her hands twitch. She pried open her eyes and saw the blurry outline of a face. A low, soft voice spoke, but the sound was muffled. Tori swallowed the large, sour lump in her throat. She licked her dry lips and tried to sit up. Something shoved her back down, and her head thudded against the floor.

The sensation of someone straddling her sent goosebumps across her chilled flesh. A sharp slap stung her face, and she bolted up. Stringy hair brushed against her skin as she sat.

Tori blinked a couple of times and let the bottle slip from her grip. Her knuckles ached. Something breathed softly inches from her face. The features of a face appeared. A bushy eyebrow. A doe-brown eye framed by a fringe of lashes. A soft, pink cheek. The curve of a smile materialized. Tori scrambled backward.

A teenage girl sat in front of her, knees tucked into her chest. She smiled. The stench of decay billowed from her.

"Surprised to see me?" the girl asked. Her grin broadened.

A writhing tangle wriggled in Tori's guts. Was she awake? She felt awake, but it was hard to tell.

The girl crawled on her hands and knees to Tori's face, close enough that the jagged pain of farsightedness shot through her eyes. The stale breath hovered like the stink of an open sewer.

"You haven't had enough to drink," the girl whispered, feather-light, just next to Tori's ear, a friend sharing a secret. It was intimate enough to blow back the hair at her ear. "It's time to have more."

Tori lifted her gaze to the writing desk above her. The bottles were gone, even the airline bottles.

The girl—*was her name Lexie? For some reason, Tori thought the girl's name was Lexie*—shook her head and held up a bottle. The liquid inside was brown, but it had no label. Tori shook her head. She didn't believe she could stand up on her own. Her eyes sagged under the weight of the liquor she'd already consumed. Lexie twisted the bottle open with a *click-click* and fumes rose up into Tori's nostrils. The fragrance was sweet and delicate, like rose petals and sugar cookies. Innocuous. Comforting. Smooth on the way down. The mellowest booze, like suckling mother's milk. Tori couldn't stop guzzling it. Warmth spread down her limbs and faded into a pleasant numbness. It was like taking a punch from a prizefighter. Tori slumped backward and found herself freefalling into a black pit.

Was this death? This black pool of nothingness? Tori didn't strain against it. She wondered if she could even fight it if she tried. It was the first time in days she felt sane. It was the first time in a long time when she felt peace. She was suspended in a room so dark she strained to make out corners and walls. She rolled her head to the side in the hopes of seeing something. Lexie's soft breath was the only sound. A hand clutched her arm. Pain shot down to her elbow.

The love you need ain't gonna see you through.

"No one loves you," Lexie sing-songed. "No one loves you, no one loves you, no one loves you. And no one ever will."

A deep, low laugh followed, one so incongruous coming from a giddy, mocking teenage girl. Tori tried to talk. Her voice cracked, and the syrupy, metallic taste of blood flowed from her throat.

"Help. Me." Tori choked out the words.

A chorus of hoots and hollers rose up from the empty room, echoing in some cavernous chamber. Something white fluttered in the distance and broke through the darkness. A small child dressed in a white gown rounded the corner, strawberry blonde curls bouncing as she moved, humming a nursery rhyme song. The cotton of the gown puffed out slightly in a silent breeze. Goosebumps perked up on Tori's skin at the sight of her.

"Miss Tori?" the small child cooed. "Why did you kill Lexie?"

The child extended a hand and smoothed Tori's hair. The touch felt ephemeral and sticky like a spiderweb. Tori stared, unable to speak. The little girl's bottom lip puffed, a prelude to tears.

Voices echoed beyond them.

"Get away from her," a woman's voice scolded, severe and angry. "We don't associate with people like that. She's evil. A murderer."

The little girl recoiled, walked backward, and slid back into the nothingness. The chorus of voices rose up, accusatory and angry. A sound, like rain pattering against the window pane, started up, and Tori listened, confused about the source. An explosion of orange and black butterflies swarmed toward her. They hummed and zigzagged out of the ether like irritated bees, and instinct compelled her to protect her face, but she couldn't move. They fluttered at her, beating against her face. Her mouth opened in shock and revulsion, and a butterfly slipped inside, its papery wings flapping against the roof of her mouth. Its spiny, hairy legs tickled her tongue and gums, and she choked. Her eyes bulged, and her hands closed into ice-cold fists as it worked its way down her gullet.

"We don't want her here," a voice rang out above the constant thrum of wings. "Why did you bring her here? She hasn't learned anything. She's a snotty, selfish, two-faced bitch. She doesn't belong here. Send her back."

Tori's heart raced. She felt pressure closing in around her. The butterfly crawled out from her mouth, and its brethren scattered away in a brilliant explosion. She stared for a minute, unable to speak, but rage bubbled up.

"Why are you torturing me?" Tori shouted, entangling her fingers in her hair. "Don't you think I've suffered enough? Yes, I killed that kid. And I live with that every fucking day. All day. Why are you judging me for the way I live with it?"

Burning tears built in her sinuses and snot flowed from her nose. She swiped at the gunk with the back of her hand and pressed her eye sockets with her fingers. When she looked up again, she was sitting in the bedroom. Had she ever left? She'd never felt happier to be alone.

The empty bottle on the floor gleamed in the lamplight, and she clutched it. She shook the final drops onto her tongue. The dregs settled on her mouth and tasted like creamy, sweet mocha.

Tori had to do something. They were getting to her, worming their way beneath her skin.

She couldn't shake the vision of the woman who had attacked her at the bar, that Perez woman. She tortured Tori, and she couldn't even begin to imagine what she might be capable of. Tori didn't even know what was real anymore, but she believed this was the goal of the slithering being that lived in her head. She closed her eyes and saw two red, glowing orbs, like twin cigarettes burning, and she knew it was this woman.

She flopped onto the sunken mattress and drew the down comforter up to her forehead, wondering why the liquor wasn't working anymore. Her body trembled again in longing for more, but she knew one more drink would probably finish her off. She lay, sweat rolling from every pore in her body. Her underwear was soaked through—not from urine, but from dripping sweat. What she wanted was another bath, something to rinse the fine film of sweat from her body. She couldn't possibly try the bathroom in her suite again. The snakes could be waiting just inside the faucet.

Horror clutched her at the thought of going back into the communal bathroom on the second floor. The thought of watching her father step, bloated and putrid, into the shower stall made her grab the blankets and pull them tightly around her body.

The thing squirming in her body shouted obscenities into her ear. It was angry, and it banged around until Tori's head throbbed. Her body folded in half at the waist and she rolled onto her side. She vomited onto the plush comforter.

Something clunked its way upstairs, and Liquid sloshed as the weight of an unexpected visitor ascended the stairs and halted at the suite door. Tori screamed and her entire body quivered. She shoved herself up and launched herself out of the bed. Glass clanked against the wall. She saw a shadow on the bare walls of the stairwell. Amelia kicked the door open. Blood trickled from a gaping wound framed by blacked, matted hair. Ice shot through Tori's veins. Amelia clutched two bottles. One was a blood-smeared Bombay bottle. The other was a rich brown bottle of Maker's Mark, its red wax dripping like its own massive head wound.

Amelia stepped into the center of the room. Her eyes burned with rage, but she said nothing. The silence horrified Tori more than any gore.

Amelia didn't flutter like a ghost. She offered no evidence of her demise. She stood, solid as ever, holding out both bottles as an offering.

The thing in Tori's body writhed and smashed itself against her guts. All the breath left her lungs. Amelia drew closer, a zombie with two boozy sacrifices.

Drink.

Drink.

Drink.

Before long, the house's restless spirits rattled windows. They shook so violently, Tori threw her arms over her face in anticipation of them shattering. They all chanted, like some fraternity hazing a pledge.

Amelia stood just over her. A clotted red blob fell onto Tori's foot. Tori looked up. Amelia's mouth was a slit. Her eyes glowed with fury, but she held those bottles inches from Tori's face, insistent.

Tori clutched the gin bottle first, cracked it open, and chugged it so hard, the liquid hurt her throat. Liquor blew up through her nose, burning her sinuses. Three-quarters of the way through the bottle, gin spewed from her puffed cheeks. Still, she gulped.

The empty bottle thudded when it hit the floor.

Amelia shoved the Maker's Mark at her. Tori shook her head and gasped, desperate to catch her breath. Sweat poured from the top of her head. Her stomach heaved and sloshed.

She clutched the bottle. The sight of the brown liquor made her want to throw up, but the squirming presence that lived beneath her skin forced her to peel back the seal and put it to her lips.

The bourbon felt like velvet on her tongue until everything

went numb. The oaky, vanilla spiciness of the booze cut through the overwhelming vapor rising into her nostrils. She tried to pull the bottle away from her mouth, but something forced it back. She couldn't take anymore. Vomit caught in her throat, and she struggled to swallow the booze being forced down her gullet. Tears gushed from her eyes as she tried to breathe. Finally, the bottle smashed against the floor, and a torrent of vomit flowed from her mouth. Chunks of some indeterminate food plopped out. Once all the food was gone, blood spewed out instead.

Tori sat in the puddles beneath her and curled into a ball. Her belly groaned with pain. Her body quaked.

Amelia, now empty-handed, staggered forward and slumped to the floor. Tori tried to scream, but acrid vomit scorched her throat and she couldn't.

Her entire body felt depleted and sucked dry. She tried to push herself up but skidded on the thick conglomeration of vomit and blood. She hefted herself up on wobbly legs and moved to the bathroom. She took an upside down, paper-covered glass from the soap dish, filled it with tap water, and slugged it down like she'd been trapped for a month in the desert. Seconds later, it poured from her throat, tinged pink with blood.

A thick, cottony bubble built in her throat. All she wanted was to wash it down. She glugged down another glass of water, but it gurgled back up.

Her heart thudded at her jaw. She pressed her fingers into the bed frame. Dizziness overwhelmed her, and her knees buckled. A blur swirled around her. Something roared in her ears. A white blob at the corner of her eye caught her attention. She turned her head, but vomited thick globs of blood onto the hardwood. She put a hand to her gummy, sweaty forehead and pushed herself along the wall until the white blob came into focus. It was the antique phone on the bedside table.

She picked up the receiver and pressed 9-1-1. It *brrrrrr*ed, a soothing sound in her throbbing ears.

"Nine-one-one. Your emergency is not important at all to us. You should eat shit and die."

The voice on the other end was cold and metallic. "Help. Me."

Tori couldn't hear herself say the words. Her voice barely choked out the plea.

"Ma'am, this line is for emergencies only. A dying drunk bitch is *not* an emergency."

The dial tone buzzed. Boiling fluid built up in her throat, and a rush of lava-hot blood bubbled out.

The overwhelming desire to live clutched her. She gripped the bedside table and dragged herself out of the bedroom and down the stairs, clenching the banister until her fingers ached. She slumped against the wall and lurched, one leg at a time toward the front door. After four steps, weakness pulled her down to her knees, and she crawled to the door. She stumbled out and pulled herself to the edge of the porch. She vaulted herself over the edge and tumbled, head over feet. A crack ripped down her back as she flipped against the sharp edges of each step all the way to the street below.

Tori's face pressed against the hard asphalt. The glitter of the road came into focus against her blurred vision. Wind swept over her. She lay there, all the energy drained. Maybe this is where she would die.

The hum of an engine vibrated the ground beneath her. She tried to push herself up, but her face smashed back against the street. The vibrations grew stronger, and a dull whirr rose up in her ears. The hot air from the hood of the car bore down on her. She braced herself for the crushing roll that would disconnect her parts and smash her into the ground.

Brakes screeched, and a car door slammed closed. A scurrying sound followed and someone was at her side. This person flipped her over, and she saw the glare of streetlamps. The light shattered into a million stars just beyond. The black outline of a person's face broke into the field of light. The figure pulled at her arm, and a jolt of pain ripped down the left side of her body. The pain rippled and expanded until her entire body was a pulsing chunk of flesh. The figure hefted her into its arms. Her savior's torso smelled like laundry detergent and fast food French fries. For some reason, the smell of food sparked memories of her childhood visits. Her dad might've been lifting her, exhausted and sunburned after a day on the beach, into the car. They'd just picked up a basket of hot, salty fries from a boardwalk stand, and she would eat them in the backseat as they drove away. She inhaled it on the mysterious person she now relied upon for her life, and those smells engulfed her until her muscles released. She felt herself flop backwards. Something drained from her mouth.

Faint sounds and movements whirled. The engine rumbled. Night breezed by. Colors in negative blurred against the windshield. The roadway rocked her. Someone pulled her again, this time slamming her against something white and soft. A needle jammed into her skin, and everything twinkled. Blinking lights exploded in her vision. Voices droned. Her ears perked, and she tried to understand, but the words all sounded like gibberish.

Her eyes strained to open. She felt the presence of someone at her side, and she wanted to see who it was. Each time she tried to open her eyes, they fluttered shut again. Once, she saw the outline, a shadowy flutter of cloth against metal. She tried again. Something oozed down from the cloth, and she clamped her eyes shut. Before long, she drifted into the darkness behind her eyelids.

CHAPTER 15

Chris's body ached. Roughing up Mr. Ramones had taken a greater toll on him than he realized. His lower back was stiff, and he rubbed the spot with his arthritic fingers. There was a time he could go to a convention and come home feeling energized and refreshed. Tonight, he felt like he could crash into bed. The microwave beeped, and the *rattle* of popping popcorn ceased. He grabbed his dinner and headed for the living room. Boxes of comics sat unmoved in his trunk, but he sank into his recliner and dipped his hand into the warm popcorn bag.

There was an old *Twilight Zone* episode on television, and he cranked up the volume.

"Oh, cool. 'The Hitchhiker.' I love this one."

He grabbed a handful of popcorn and stuffed the buttery snack into his mouth. Inger Stevens stepped into the telephone booth and picked up the receiver to call her mother. Chris smiled. He loved this part.

Inger was such a beauty with her dimpled cheeks and fresh skin. He recalled when she died. He was a teenager then. Suicide by overdose. He'd never admit to anyone that he once considered a similar way out in the days after Margaret and Emmy died. It would have been easier than the path he ultimately chose. He was trapped in the life of a superhero, unable to stop even if he wanted to. When he saw someone in peril, it was an automatic change. He didn't need to change in a phone booth or spin in a circle or even pull open his button-up to reveal some QS in bright primary colors emblazoned upon his undershirt. QuickSilver was emblazoned upon his soul. After thirty-five years of leaping tall buildings in a single bound, you'd think he'd have earned a break by now.

A thunderous knock rattled his door, and he jumped up, knocking the popcorn onto the floor. It scattered into places he'd probably never think to clean.

His knees wobbled at the intrusion, but he lurched to the door. A police officer stood on the other side, holding a notepad.

"Mr. Silver?" he asked.

Chris nodded and said, "How can I help you, officer?"

His stomach sank at the thought of Mr. Ramones pressing assault charges. Doug warned him. If only he could've stopped himself.

"I need to ask you a few questions. May I come in?"

Chris grimaced and pulled the door open the rest of the way.

"Sure. Come on in. I apologize for the mess. Your knock startled me, and I dropped my snack."

The officer gave him a puzzled look and shrugged.

"Do you happen to know a blonde woman, about five foot six inches tall, approximately 140 pounds?"

It was Chris's turn to adopt a puzzled look.

"I can't think of anyone I know matches that description. I wish I did know a woman who looks like that," he laughed nervously.

"Mr. Silver, we found your business card in her back pocket."

A chill worked its way up from Chris's feet. The word *found* rattled him.

"Found? Is this woman in some sort of trouble?"

"She's very ill and in the hospital. She was almost hit by a truck earlier this evening. She had no identification on her, and when we searched her clothing, we pulled your business card from her back pocket. We visited your store, and one of your employees told us you were home."

The relief Chris felt that this police visit wasn't about Mr. Ramones dissipated and was replaced by the terror that someone out there needed him. His mind raced when he thought back on the people who had taken cards at WildCon. He'd placed a cardholder on his exhibitor table. God only knew how many people grabbed one while browsing or breezing through. Then he remembered. The last card he'd given out was at the Nail before he left for Wildwood.

"Officer, is this woman's hair long and dark blonde?"

The policeman nodded.

"Can you tell me what happened to her?" Chris asked, starting to put the pieces together.

The officer looked like this line of questioning was getting on his nerves.

"I'm afraid I can't get into details with you, Mr. Silver. Do you know this woman or not?"

"I think I know who you're talking about. Would I be able to come down to the hospital with you and see her? Let me ask you this. Did alcohol land her in the hospital?"

The officer's stern countenance softened a bit.

"Well, yes, as a matter of fact."

"I believe I do know this woman. I think I can help you. I'll follow you in my car."

The officer motioned toward the door, and Chris slipped his feet into a pair of shoes and grabbed his keys from the kitchen counter.

Chris climbed behind the wheel of the still-loaded Subaru, and he watched the police officer pull out of the driveway. Blue and red lights swirled, and Chris followed. The cop sped along the narrow roadway, whooshing past reeds. Chris struggled to keep up, but he knew where the hospital was. Adrenaline coursed through his veins, and his breath sped up. Panic set in, and he sniffled and huffed as tears built. The last time he'd raced behind a police car on the way to the hospital, it'd been the night the cop came to his door to tell him about Margaret and Emmy. Their faces flashed in his mind, and his shoulders shuddered. His nostrils burned as he ran red lights along with the cruiser, history repeating itself. He'd believed all those years ago that his heart would explode, and he wasn't entirely certain that wouldn't happen now.

The cruiser pulled into the hospital parking garage, and Chris smeared tears away from his cheeks. He pulled in behind and waited for the boom barrier to lift and let the cop move forward.

The cop car edged ahead. Chris took a ticket, and the boom barrier lifted again. He watched the cop pull into a spot, and he found one a few spaces away. He put the car in park, pulled down the visor, and flipped up the mirror. He studied his eyes for signs of tears and wiped away a few stray ones.

He climbed out and ran to catch up to the officer, who was already marching briskly toward the emergency entrance. The two men walked in silence and got into the elevator. At the sixth floor, they got out and moved to Room 627.

Something beeped incessantly. He didn't even notice the woman at first. She was buried beneath intertwined tubes and wires. Her hair was matted to her face, which was bleached of all its color. Her blue lips framed a large tube that jutted into her throat. Machines whirred.

Was this the woman he'd seen at the bar? She looked like a

ghost, especially wrapped under layers of white hospital sheets. Chris studied her features. She had smooth, flat cheeks and a perky nose. Her hair might have been dark blonde, but she was soaked through with sweat, so he couldn't tell for sure. The smell coming from her, however, was undeniable. Alcohol bursting from her pores. It smelled like fermented fruit and the watery mess that sometimes collects at the bottom of the garbage can. There was no denying that smell. This woman almost drank herself to death.

"Alcohol poisoning?" Chris asked the cop, who stood on the other side of the woman and stared down at her.

"Hmmm? Oh. Yeah. Worst case I've seen. She's lucky. Staggered out into the street. Some guy in a truck nearly took her out. Nearly shit myself when her BAC came in—0.8. Had enough in her blood to kill at least three people. I don't see how she survived the trip to the emergency room."

Chris's face flushed.

"I think she's a woman I saw at the Rusty Nail the other night. I'm afraid I never caught her name, but you might want to try Bracken Nunnally. He was working the bar when she was there."

The cop flipped open his notebook and jotted down the name.

"Thanks. I'll give him a call. You're free to go."

"Officer, do you think it would be all right if I stayed? I hate to think that this poor woman will be up here all by herself. At least until you can reach a relative."

The cop shrugged.

"Suit yourself. If the hospital staff tells you to leave, you'll need to obey their orders."

Chris gave a smile that turned down at the corners of his mouth.

Tori woke surrounded by white. She clutched at some tubes jutting from her arms and winced at the jab of pain from the IV in her hand. Someone was in the room with her, but she couldn't make out the form. Time was a vague matter. There was no way to tell how long she'd been out or if it was morning, afternoon, or night. Her vision blurred, and her head felt fuzzy. Turning her head seemed like it took all the energy stored in her body.

A face loomed, nose-to-nose. A lightning bolt shot down her spine as she jerked up. The curve of the cheek. The black eyes were wild and crazed, lined deeply with wrinkles. A furious vertical line split the eyebrows. A smile, devoid of any happiness, stretched preternaturally across the face.

Don't you want a drink? It's been a whole day since you drank. The voice growled into her ears.

"Hello? Are you all right?"

A man's voice rose up from somewhere in the room.

Tori closed her eyes and opened them again. The face that had hovered so close was gone. Her vision remained foggy. Lights glared, and it hurt to look at them. Like some strange, dream-fueled concert, lyrics popped into her mind. *Telephone line, give me some time.*

She sensed that the man sat on the far end of the room, beyond the curtain that separated her bed from the other one. Metal-on-metal scraped, and the curtain opened.

A featureless face appeared just inside. A hand touched her own.

"Tori?"

It was Bracken's voice. She jerked back her hand as if she'd been bitten by a snake.

The love you need ain't gonna see you through.

Words gurgled in her throat, angry words she would've shouted. That he was a liar and a scumbag. That he had a lot of fucking nerve to show up now after leading her on like that. But she couldn't speak. The boiling-hot fluid gurgling in her throat kept her from ripping into him. It took her a moment to realize a plastic tube blocked her from moving her mouth.

Her eyelids fluttered open. A beeping sound rose up in her ears, and the space between beeps shortened.

"Hey, you're awake. I hope you don't mind that I came. Chris Silver spent the whole day here with you, but he had to run home real quick. The cops called me this morning and told me they needed me to identify you. Lady, you scared the shit out of me. I even went back to the Seaside when I couldn't reach you on the phone, and I saw what a mess the place was. What the hell happened, Tori? Why did you do this to yourself? I tried to call Amelia, but she must be out of town. Sometimes, her mother-in-law needs help, and she has to leave quickly."

Amelia?

"Anyway, listen. I don't know what happened last night. I don't know what was going through your mind. And I felt like I ... I don't know. I guess I felt really guilty for what happened between us. That was a dick move on my part, and I'm sorry. That's all, really. I'm sorry. I hope you don't mind, but the officer was able to track down your mom in Exeter. She can't make it down, but the officer promised to keep her posted on your condition. I don't know how much of this is getting through to you, but I'm worried about you."

The door clicked and timid footsteps clacked against the floor.

Tori anticipated the visitor as they brushed against the curtain. The bandage on his cheek came into focus first. A tall man with silver hair and a salt-and-pepper beard peeked around the curtain. Tori sat up straighter, tangling herself further in the mess of wires. Pain shot through her legs.

"Victoria?"

A fragrance, wood smoke and apples and cotton cloth, swirled around him, and she knew it was the man who'd given her his business card when she drank without a care at the bar. She wondered if it was her Chris Silver.

"So glad to see you're awake. I was here overnight, but I needed to get a shower and change into some new clothes. The nurse told me you'd probably be out for a while. Oh, I'm sorry. I guess I should introduce myself. I'm Chris. Chris Silver. Gotta say, you gave me quite a scare last night."

He had a lopsided smile with a dimple on the right side. He may have had one on the left, but the large bandage was probably covering it. His chocolate eyes were framed by long lashes. Sometimes, when he blinked, the lashes fluttered against the skin below his eyes. The specks of silver hair gleamed in the overbearing fluorescent lights. His presence comforted her, and she wished she could get Bracken to leave, but she couldn't communicate that desire. She pawed at the tube, hoping someone might remove it for her.

Chris reached over her head and buzzed for the nurse. A few minutes later, a woman in a white uniform breezed in.

"Everything okay? Does she need anything?"

"I think she wants that tube removed. She's trying to talk," Chris said.

The nurse studied her. She pulled a flashlight out of her uniform pocket and tracked it back and forth. Pain shot through

Tori's eyes, and she blinked.

"I'll have to bring the doctor in before we can remove anything. That's his call. She does look better. Let me go grab him, and we'll see what our next steps are."

The nurse left, and Tori felt the tremors roiling beneath her skin.

It's been a while since you last had a drink. Isn't it about time for another?

It was still inside her, worming, snaking, taunting. Her head pulsated. The sound of the door clicking open hammered her skull. She put a hand to it and drew back a palm dampened with sweat from her hair.

The doctor, a short, squat guy with a receding hairline, flipped through her chart and made a series of grunts and hums. He glanced at her over the clipboard.

"Well, welcome back to the world of the living," he said.

Flashbacks of the horrors she saw the night before in that dark, restless place made the words crawl down her skin. He approached the bedside and pulled the curtain around them, blocking out Chris Silver and Bracken.

"All right now. This won't hurt, but you might vomit." He turned to the nurse and said, "Can we get a pan over here, just to be safe?"

He twisted something connected to the tube and pulled. Tori felt it leave her trachea, and the hot liquid built up inside her throat spewed forth. The nurse pushed the metal pan under her chin, and yellow, putrid-smelling fluid flowed into it.

"Mmmm," the doctor said. "Always delightful."

Tori already despised him. His words sounded snarky and irritated her like the itch in the center of her back that she just couldn't reach.

"So, how long have you been an alcoholic?" he asked.

She coughed so hard her throat ached, and a blot of blood spattered on the white sheet covering her. Tori would've throttled him if she'd had the strength. How dare he?

She tried her voice.

"I'm." The word came out hoarse and strained. "Not."

His lip lifted into a lopsided smile that made her irrationally angry. Her face burned, and she wanted him to leave. She could breathe fine on her own now, and she wanted out.

"Why don't you get her some water?" he said to the nurse. "Looks like she should be all right. And when you're ready to admit you have a problem, there are plenty of programs that can help. I'd like to observe you another day, and then you're free to go home."

She wanted to say something else, but the acrid burn in her throat prevented it. He pulled the curtain back.

Bracken nervously edged his way to the bed.

"Is she going to be okay?" he asked the doctor.

The doctor raised his hands up in despair.

"This time, sure. Next time, I don't know. There might be permanent liver damage already. She looks remarkably healthy all things considered. And that's probably the most concerning thing of all. She's developed a tolerance. All I can say is that the next several days are probably going to be her worst nightmare."

Tori resented that he was talking about her as if she wasn't even there. He turned to leave, and she relaxed a little, but Bracken's presence aggravated and humiliated her. She just wanted to be left alone. Genuine shame scorched her that anyone had seen her this way but especially that he had. The nurse followed him out.

Bracken looked like a man who'd just pissed his pants—and

the piss was rapidly cooling.

"Hey, listen. I should really get going. I picked up a couple of things from Amelia's place. I'm glad you're feeling better. If you need anything, I left my phone number on the table over there."

He bent at the waist and kissed her cheek. Her hand swatted at him involuntarily.

Chris pulled a gauche-looking mauve chair next to her bed.

"Are you going to be okay?" he asked, his voice low and soft. It cooled the fiery burn under her skin.

"Yeah. I think so," she said. It still hurt to talk.

"I think I'm going to stay. If you don't mind, that is. I've got nothing planned, and you seem like you could use a friend."

Tori licked her dry lips and smiled. The delicate skin cracked at the small movement.

"Were you the one who saved me?" she asked.

Chris's eyebrows furrowed.

"No. The guy who almost hit you with his truck brought you to the hospital ..."

"That's not what I mean. Your shop. It was on Beach, like a long, long time ago, like back in the early 80s, right?"

Chris leaned forward. "Yes, that's right. How'd you know that?"

"Do you remember, there were these little shits. They chased me." A rattling cough erupted from her chest. "These two kids. I was wearing a bikini. Hell, I didn't even have anything to put in the bikini. I was just a little kid. And they chased after me, and you stopped them."

Chris shook his head. "I'm sorry, I don't know what you're talking about. Do you want a drink of water?"

Tori held up her hand. "I know it was you. You told me to come in for a *Wonder Woman* number three-hundred. But I never did get to come in, because Mom was pissed off at Dad for getting shitfaced in public again, and we went home not long after that. You walked me back to the beach."

A light flickered in Chris's eyes.

"My God," he said. "I do remember that. I can't believe you do. That must've been, oh, 1983. That was when *Wonder Woman* three-hundred came out. Yeah, my shop was on Beach, and I remember that little girl."

He stared into space for a few seconds, and Tori watched a tear trickle down his face. He brushed it away with the back of his knuckle and snickered at his own emotions.

"I guess sometimes you never realize how your actions stay with someone," he said.

Chris extended his hand, and Tori clutched it, feeling a beam of warmth just like she had walking back to the beach more than thirty years earlier.

"Can you help me now?" she muttered. "I don't want to die."

His bear paw of a hand swallowed her own, and he gave her a tight-lipped smile.

"Yes," was all he said.

CHAPTER 16

Pain jagged down Chris's neck. He propped himself up on his elbows and rolled himself off of the folding chairs. The room was still dark. Monitors beeped. The door creaked open, and a nurse eased inside. Tori slept, a halo of recessed lighting framing her features. Her face glowed a sickly white.

The nurse silently took down vitals from the monitor. Tori's eyes fluttered open, and she and the nurse exchanged muted words. Tori opened her mouth and took a thermometer. Next, she extended an arm for a blood pressure cuff. There were more muffled words, and the nurse shuffled back out of the room. Tori rolled onto her side and caught sight of Chris looking at her.

"Sorry," he said. "Just couldn't get comfortable."

"Why don't you just go home?" she asked. "You don't have to stay here all night."

He shook his head and smoothed her hair away from her forehead, a fatherly gesture. "You're looking so much better. I'll bet they'll discharge you in the morning. You're going to need a ride."

Her eyes widened. "I don't have anywhere to go," she confessed.

"Will you stay with me? I can get you some help."

"I doubt you can help me," she said. "It's probably best if you don't get involved."

Chris felt the adrenaline stir.

"Of course I can help. You need some rest, some good nutrition, and someone to get you to AA every day."

"I don't have a ..."

"Listen, lady. You almost died. Don't tell me you don't have a drinking problem."

Chris felt the heat rise from his Nighthawk T-shirt. He wondered for a moment if he was getting himself in over his head, but QuickSilver was coming to the forefront again. It was like a freight train gaining speed on a track. He couldn't push it back once it started. All he could do was flow with it and do his best to help. Logically, he knew this woman was probably trouble. Logic did not play into the life of a hero. Still, he tempered himself and took a breath.

"I want to help," he said. "Besides, who else do you have? I have a spare bedroom. You can stay there until you dry out, but my rules are non-negotiable. You go to AA every day."

Tori's head fell back against the pillow. Her shoulders rocked up and down. He feared he might've made her cry until he noticed her forearms were also jerking up and down. Her chest followed, and before long, her whole body quaked and convulsed. Chris lunged up and pressed the call button for the nurse. She ran into the room and saw Tori pitching up and down in the bed. She darted back out. Tori's eyelids flickered up to reveal only the whites. Seconds ticked by, but it felt like an eternity as he watched foam bubble up from her lips.

The door slammed open, and the nurse brought in a crew of white-clad people who set about checking monitors and injecting clear liquids into her IV and holding her steady as muscles clenched and tensed. A man in all white grabbed Chris by the shoulder and escorted him out of the room.

"Sir, I'm afraid you'll have to leave the room now. You can sit in the waiting area. Someone will be out to update you shortly."

Chris's stomach sank. He rounded the corner and saw a few people sitting in reception area chairs. A television suspended on a metal arm displayed Dr. Phil's disdainful frown. A woman wept in front of him, and he scowled. The caption below read: YOU CAN FOOL YOURSELF, BUT YOU CAN'T FOOL ME. GET REAL. THE FIRST STEP TO GETTING HELP IS ADMITTING YOU HAVE A PROBL—

Chris turned away and paced in front of the bank of windows on the far side of the waiting room. There was nothing else to do now.

A swarm fluttered around her in the dark place. Voices swirled in the ether, hushed under the thrum of batting wings. They threw invectives at her like stones.

The weight of butterflies crushed her chest, and she struggled to take a breath. Tori felt herself slipping. She closed her eyes, and the pressure released. Her eyes flicked open, and she watched a bespectacled face move in front of her own. A receding hairline glowed in the overhead lights. The lights looked like giant, white eyes reflected in the lenses of his glasses. A straight slit of a mouth curled into a smile.

"She's a lost cause," the man said. It was that smart-ass doctor from yesterday. "Let's just give up. She's not even worth the effort."

A laugh, sharp and bitter, cracked in her ears. Other voices were there, too, both male and female, and they joined in a chorus of laughter.

"You're right, Dr. Ellison. Why waste our time? It's not like she's going to stop drinking. I guarantee you, she wants a drink right now."

The words resonated in her head. She wanted a drink. She would've wrenched herself up, pulled out all the wires that tethered her to the bed, shoved aside all the people working on her, and walked barefoot to Harrington's Liquors for a bottle of *anything*. They were right. She didn't deserve to be saved. She couldn't even argue.

The doctor's face faded into the blackness and was replaced by another face—this one so familiar, it froze her blood. The woman gave her a happy wave, extended her middle finger, and pressed it against her lips in a kiss.

"See you in Hell, bitch," the angry, metallic voice growled.

A spark within Tori refused to go out. She focused on coming out, resisting the saturating pull of the dark room until it began to turn gray at the edges like the beginnings of sunrise; forms like aliens prodding and poking her moved into focus. A beeping sound rose up. A light stabbed at her eyes, and the man with the receding hairline clutched the sides of her mouth with his fingers, pressing her lips into a squishy lump.

"I think she's coming around. Heart rate?"

"Forty-five and rising."

"BP?"

Something squeezed her arm, huffed, and *hissed*.

"Ninety over sixty."

"She's not out of the woods yet, but I think she'll make it."

The beeping became steadier and stronger. The voices in her

head went quiet, and she breathed deeply. Her head sank into the stiff hospital pillow, and she slept.

CHAPTER 17

Tori pulled on the sweater Chris brought for her to wear home. The shirt she'd been admitted in was ripped and covered in road grit. Chris's navy blue sweater sagged past her fingertips and fell around her knees. She resembled a small child dressed in Dad's clothing.

"You about ready?" he asked.

She nodded. "Yeah. Whenever you are. Listen, I can't thank you enough for this. For everything. I'm ready to get sober. I never want to end up like this again."

He clutched her shoulder and led her out the hospital room door.

The ride home was quiet, too quiet, and Chris flipped on the radio to the sports station to hear the Nets score. He clicked it back off once his curiosity was satisfied and cleared his throat.

Tori expected him to say something, but he never did. They passed a convenience store at an intersection, and he clicked on the turn signal. Bud Light and Coors neon glowed in the store's windows. Thirst overcame her. The gaping maw opened up, and her arm quivered with the familiar urge. Chris made a left onto a crushed gravel road, and the car shuddered along, past briny marshes, cattails, and reeds. The lighthouse loomed in the distance. She could see it if they crested a hill but lost sight of it when they made a right and pulled into Chris's driveway.

The house was small but tidy. It had a brick façade and a small, withered garden in the front. A bloodied zombie gnome clutched its way out of the ground near the porch steps. Cute if a bit creepy, she thought, clutching her purse close to her torso.

He jogged up the stairs ahead of her and unlocked the door.

"Excuse the mess," he said. "Make yourself at home."

She stepped inside. The place was dark and dingy. Soda cans were stacked on the coffee table. Popcorn littered the floor, spilling out from an upended bag.

"Come on. I'll show you to your room. It's a little sparse."

She followed him down a narrow hallway to an empty room painted dusky pink.

"Well, where should I ..."

"Oh, don't worry," he interrupted. "I have an air mattress. Just have to get it pumped up. We can bring your stuff in later. Don't worry."

Tori gave him a pained smile. He was kind. Too kind, really, but she couldn't hide the disappointment at the accommodations. Still, she wondered what her alternatives might be. She had no idea if the cops were looking for her. She had no idea where Amelia was for that matter. The thought sent a shiver down her spine.

"Do you want to maybe try going to an AA meeting today?"

Tori was still scanning the bare room. The carpet was baby-shit green. The sliding closet displayed a spaghetti intersection of multicolored crayon and marker scribbles.

"I'm really tired," she said. "I just don't think I can do this today. If you could show me where that mattress is, I could just grab it. I need some rest."

Chris shuffled off to a closet in the hallway and returned with the flaccid air mattress, its pump dangling along behind.

"I'll set you up," he said. "Why don't you go sit down in the living room? I'll have this done in a few minutes."

She took a deep breath. The shakes were more persistent now.

It's time, you disgusting sack of shit. Go take your medicine.

It was the first time she'd heard the voice since she was at the hospital in the dark place. For a while, she thought this nightmare might finally be over. Something slimed inside her, but it felt softer, more subdued.

"If it's okay with you, I might go take a walk," she called as the electric air pump cranked up. "I could really use the fresh air."

Tori pulled her purse onto her shoulder and rushed out the front door before she could hear his response. It was far colder than she realized, and she tucked her frozen fingers into the knit of the sweater sleeves and crossed her arms under the breasts. The wind whipped through her body. Her teeth chattered.

The gravel road crunched beneath her sneakers. The reeds rattled as she scurried by. Something slithered in the water by the roadside, and she sped up, terrified that something might leap out of the marsh and pounce on her. The air changed, and the heavy sensation of someone following her pressed upon her. She hooked a right and speed-walked, retracing the path back to the convenience store.

The road narrowed, and claustrophobia grasped her. Water trickled in the marsh, melding with the lazy *swoosh* of animals moving beyond the curtain of brittle plant life. She scrambled forward, shuffling her feet as she walked. Soon, a stitch in her side made her slow and press her palm against her ribs. Breath came in sharp, shallow bursts as the shadow of something inched its way toward her. Tori saw a black blur in her peripheral vision, and she battled every instinct to turn and see what it was. Instead, she jerked forward. She could see the store's sign—Williamson's Bait 'n Tackle. The road ahead of her was completely engulfed in a shadow. Her chest tightened. A long, languid appendage reached out for her, and she ran. Sweat gathered at the small of her back. She turned and cried out at the image of a wriggling mass of snakes, knotted into a single undulating form.

The bait and tackle were her sanctuary. Her feet slapped the pavement as she zoomed past the outdoor ice freezer. A cowbell *clonk-clonked* when she shoved open the door. Tori pressed her face against the glass, staring back at the road. Nothing was there. Something brushed against her shoulder, and she wheeled around, nearly knocking into a man in a flannel shirt and dirty jeans.

"Can I help you with something, Miss? You okay?"

Tori swallowed hard and wiped the sweat from her upper lip with the back of her hand.

"I'm fine. I'll be fine. Sorry. Just thought someone was following me. But I was wrong."

The man cocked an eyebrow at her and moved to his station behind the cluttered counter. He looked like he might be ready to grab the shiny black phone and call the cops, but he didn't. The place smelled the jelly shoes she had when she was six. Wrigglers and hooks lined the display next to the register. Styrofoam containers of live worms were stacked along a wood panel wall. The coolers were in the back. That's all Tori needed. She marched past shelves of salty snacks and beyond rows of candy bars. The silver packages of Zero bars caught her eye. She turned away from them, the shuddering desire to drink overpowering any tender nostalgia she might have felt on another day.

The beer would have to do. Tori didn't much care for it. Liquor was more efficient. She hefted up two six packs of Corona. She'd spent a few Cinco de Mayos at the Carriage House, drinking Coronas with lime wedges with her associates. It would do.

The beers rattled as they gently smacked against her legs on the way back to the counter. The flannel-shirted guy banged numbers into the cash register.

"That'll be $19.05," he said.

She fished a twenty out of her billfold and passed it over to him. The change scraped in the drawer as he plucked out ninety-five cents and handed it to her. She tossed it haphazardly in the purse, desperate to crack open a beer. Shit. She'd need something to open them with. She pulled a plastic opener from a rack and slid it across the counter.

"Fifty cents," the clerk said.

Tori rattled around in her bag, took out a couple of quarters, handed them over, and dashed back into the biting cold afternoon. Silence enveloped her. She sat on the gritty concrete and pulled a cold beer from the cardboard carton.

Her hands trembled as she fumbled with the red plastic opener. She pressed the flat edge against the bottle cap and pushed up. The beer hissed like a snake, and she almost dropped it. The cap popped off, and she guzzled it, nursing from it like a baby. Half was gone before she realized it. She came up for air, gasping, and took another pull, desperate to get as much into her blood as she could.

Tori drained the last, sudsy drops from the bottle and set it aside on the concrete next to her. Her hands still trembled, almost as badly as they had when she arrived at the store. She cracked open a second beer and pulled hard on it, taking down the mild, watery beverage. It was like sucking down water.

The sun cast long shadows over the store by the time she polished off the very last beer. She'd been gone since around lunchtime, and she knew Chris would be wondering where she'd gotten to.

The clerk shoved open the door and stuck his head out, clanking the bell as he did.

"Excuse me, Miss. I'm afraid you're gonna have to leave. And take your mess with you." He eyed the empties with the kind of disdain church ladies reserve for scantily clad women.

Tori stood and felt remarkably fresh and stable.

"Sorry," she said, stooping to gather up the bottles and toss them into a stained green trashcan.

Tori gathered up her purse and headed back down the road. The marsh buzzed and hummed with life. The tension she'd felt earlier dissipated into a smooth indifference. What difference did it make if she walked right down the center of the road? If a car hit her, would it matter? Would it be justice? Her head spun, and the idea seemed genuinely funny. Uproarious laughter sputtered out of her until her eyes watered and she had to stop and put her hands on her knees. At least it would all be over. She fell to her knees, hopeful someone would come by doing about sixty in the thirty-five zone and smash her into the pavement like a cracked, battered turtle.

Good. Now you're talkin'.

The voice made her jump up and leap forward, step lively, and check her back. The memory of the massive mountain of snakes shook her.

Tori almost felt sober by the time she reached Chris's house. She was certain she could pass for sober anyway. She knocked on the door, and he answered, a concerned grimace imprinted upon his face. He opened it and let her inside.

"Where on earth have you been? I was just about to get in my car and come looking for you."

Tori shrugged. "I told you, I just needed some fresh air. So, I took a long walk."

His eyes flashed with anger. "You've been drinking." He pointed a finger in her face. "I told you, you need help. You need …"

A knocking sound startled her, and she spun around. Chris brushed past her and opened it again. Amelia stood on the other side. Tori felt the room tilt as she fell forward. Everything went dark.

Muffled voices spoke as she came around. The sight of Amelia sitting on the threadbare sofa, sipping something from a cracked mug made her dizzy again.

"Hey, you okay?" Chris asked, setting down his own mug.

Tori put a hand to her forehead. It ached.

"How?" she asked. "Where have you been?"

Amelia put her cup on the littered coffee table and leaned forward.

"You got very belligerent with me when I asked you to leave, and I felt like you were going to harm me. So, I spent a few days with my in-laws. I didn't want any trouble with you. I didn't want you to get into any trouble. So, I felt it was in everyone's best interest if I just got out of the way for a few days and let things settle down."

Tori wanted to shake her and ask her how she could possibly be here when she should, by all logic, be dead right now. She'd seen her. Hadn't she? Her mouth felt like it was stuffed with cotton, so she shut it again and kept the dreadful act to herself. Even half-drunk, she knew better than to incriminate herself.

"I heard you had an accident, and Bracken Nunnally from the Rusty Nail told me you were probably going to stay with Chris, so I came by to check on you. I didn't mean to scare you. I brought some of your things over. I hope you don't mind that I went through your stuff, but I thought you might want some extra clothes."

Tori sat up on the floor and pulled her knees into her chest. She noticed her suitcase by the front door. It comforted her to know she wouldn't have to go back to the B&B.

"Not at all," she replied. "I appreciate it. Look, I don't remember what happened the day you asked me to leave. I wasn't in my right mind, and I'm really sorry. I don't expect you to forgive me now, but I hope one day, we can at least talk about it. Because, boy, do I have a doozy of a story."

Amelia picked up her mug and took a long drink. "Chris told me what happened."

Tori shot him a bitter look.

"I want to help. That's all I was trying to do by getting you to go to AA," Amelia went on. "I swear, I wasn't trying to hurt you in any way. I suppose I can't force you, but I'm offering my help if you want it."

Amelia put the mug back on the table and stood. "Anyway, that's all. I think I'm going to head home. It's getting late, and I could use some rest."

Chris walked her to the door and let her out. They exchanged a few words Tori couldn't hear, and he closed the door behind her.

"We need to talk," he said. He clasped her hand and pulled her to her feet. She thought he was going to embrace her, but instead, he led her to the couch Amelia had been sitting on and moved to the recliner.

He sat and put his head in his hands.

"I'm an alcoholic," he told her. "I'm in recovery. Have been for more than twenty years, but nothing will ever change the fact that I'm an alcoholic. You are, too. You just haven't gotten to the point of admitting it yet. I hope you can before ..."

Something hummed in her head. It drowned out some of the words he said after this, but she tried to push it away and make it shut up.

You need to drink more, it said. *This fucker doesn't know what he's talking about.*

"... when I was a young man. My daughter was only two. My wife was twenty-three, same as me ..."

Another beer would take the edge off. Look at how nervous you are. Everyone wants to lecture you, but do they know what you've been through?

Her hands were shaking again.

"... and I just couldn't handle the pain. I drank. I drank every day. By the time I got help, I couldn't start the day without a drink. If you don't get some help soon, you are going to die. The funniest thing? I completely understand why nearly dying had absolutely no affect at all on you. The addiction is everything. You won't let anything stop you. I may not even be able to stop you. And I'm no fool. You won't get help until you really want it."

Jesus H. Christ, can this guy lecture or what? Fuck. Just think. If you'd just died like a good bitch, you wouldn't have to listen to this shit right now.

"I do want help," she said, trying to drown out the voices. "I don't want to die."

She thought she meant it, but the voices were back. It

would've been easier if she'd died. She wondered why she didn't just leap in front of oncoming traffic. Or take a knife from Chris's butcher block. Or walk into the sea. And the answer was simple. There was still a spark of life. Somewhere, tucked inside the black writhing mass of evil that wound its way through her bloodstream was the real her. Flawed, yes. Self-centered, yes. Human, yes. But also ambitious. Also intelligent. Also passionate. Also determined. She'd done a horrible thing and killed a young woman, but she felt genuine, heart-crushing, soul-breaking remorse. She'd tried to find comfort inside a bottle, and now she was trapped. And that thought terrified her more than the thing that wrapped itself around her.

"I think I just want to sleep. Would it be all right if I went to bed now?"

The orange remnants of day still lingered outside. It couldn't have been later than seven.

Chris shrugged with resignation. She crept past him to the makeshift bedroom. He'd pulled a flower-printed sheet over the air mattress. A flat pillow rested at one end. A green fleece blanket drooped over the edge.

She pulled the thin rope of the blinds, and they clacked on the way down. The room still glowed in a sickly umber. The mattress squished as she climbed onto it. It crinkled and groaned under her weight as she pulled the blanket up over her shoulder and settled her head onto the pillow. She wanted to sleep, but her eyes remained open and focused on the faded pink walls. Pink. Chris had been talking about a little girl and his wife. Cold horror broke over her skin as she realized this had been his daughter's room, and she was dead. She hadn't caught how his wife and child died, but it didn't matter. All that mattered was that he was a broken man who was trying to help her. Sobs shuddered her body. Her eyes burned and sagged. Before long, she slipped into a deep sleep.

CHAPTER 18

Tori jerked up from the depths of her slumber. The walls were dark. The house was quiet. Something was in the room with her. Her eyes strained to focus. Blue moonlight filtered through the closed blinds.

The dim light outlined an indistinct, twisting mass. Tori's heart lodged itself in her throat. She tried to scream, but nothing came out. Something extended toward her, long and elegant. The moonglow illuminated two black eyes and a forked tongue that zipped in and out of the being's mouth. It felt leathery against her skin and wound itself between her arms and around her waist, pulling itself taut and squeezing her tightly.

Don't worry. I'm still here, it hissed. *It's time to drink again.*

"No," she said aloud. "I don't want to. I almost died. I don't want to die. I can't do this. I can't. I won't."

Tori's mouth fell open as hot tears burned her face. She heaved up and down, desperate to suck in a breath.

"You can't make me."

The fuck I can't.

It squeezed until her eyes bulged.

Get up. Get out.

She stumbled onto the floor on her hands and knees and crawled for the door. It opened of its own volition. The snaky conglomerate marched her into the darkened house. Her feet were bare, but the thing wouldn't let her stop. The air stung her skin when she opened the front door and slipped outside. She padded down the front steps and across the frosty-cold lawn. Her feet burned.

She still wore the droopy sweater Chris had given her when she left the hospital. It hung around her body, and the wind pierced the knit. She felt like a criminal being led to the electric chair as she rounded the corner and took the right that led to the Williamson's Bait 'n Tackle. The darkness along the marshy roadway was all-consuming. Noises perked her ears. Slushing and rustling, *whoooing* and chirping. Night animals stalked and hunted, slinking a path through the brush to mice and chipmunks. Tori listened as something light and fast charged through the bushes to her left. A fox bounded in front of her. The sight startled her, but it paid her no mind, leaping full-throttle at a doomed chipmunk that cowered among the brown grass at the roadside.

Tori's lips quivered at the cold. She shuffled along, gripped by the beast, unsure of what exactly it wanted her to do. The convenience store would be closed by now. Night blanketed the neighborhood. The frigid road bit at her feet.

A light glowed ugly and yellow just down the street. The store was in sight, but how would she buy anything? Even if the place was open, she didn't have money or her purse. The grip on her waist tightened until she fell forward. The road shredded her knees. She cried out and struggled back to her feet. Blood seeped through the blue fabric of her jeans. She tried to bend to examine the scrapes, but the slick appendage drew her back upright.

The gravel of Williamson's driveway gouged the soft, tender balls of her feet. Her pace quickened, and she stepped up onto the smooth concrete walkway at the entrance.

The inside of the store was dark. The streetlamp reflected in the window, and Tori approached the glass and put a hand to it. She saw herself. Her face was long and gaunt. Hollow bowls replaced her eyes. The sides of her mouth were carved with deep lines. Her stringy hair frayed in all directions. She strained to see the beast that clutched her, but it blended into the darkness beyond her.

Footsteps crunched on the gravel, and she jerked around. A round-bellied man with an oil-stained T-shirt and dirt-coated jeans jittered toward her. He clutched a bottle in each hand. The liquid sloshed as he approached.

"Hey there, sweetheart."

Her heart lurched as she realized it was the same dirty man she'd seen at Harrington's days ago, the man whose mouth spewed snakes.

She backed up until she hit the glass.

"I don't want any trouble," she said.

A craggy laugh erupted from the man's throat. Tori could see he didn't have any front teeth, and she worried snakes might wriggle out of the chasm.

"Ain't gonna get no trouble from me, sweetheart," he chuckled. "Naw, I brought you a little something. We can share. See? I'm your friend."

He extended one of the bottles to her. The liquid inside was black like tar. He took the other, which filled with clear fluid, and suckled from it.

"Aaahhh," he said, coming up for a breath. "That hits the spot. Go ahead. Take a drink. Good for what ails ya."

Tori studied the contents of her bottle. She pulled the cork from it and inhaled vanilla, oak, and chocolate. Deeper, it smelled like Christmas. Allspice, cloves, and cinnamon. Rum, maybe, she thought. She sipped, and the flavors burst on her tongue. A hint of orange, a nip of cocoa.

"There. That's a girl. Now come on. Sit down here."

Tori followed his lead and sat on the hard concrete. The oily man took another glug. She tipped back her drink. The sweet, spicy, fragrant liquid slipped neatly down her throat.

"Are you real?" she asked. The fact that she wasn't a shuddering, terrified mess surprised her. The memory of snakes spewing forth from the man's mouth was vivid in her head.

The man wheezed when he laughed. "Do *you* think I'm real?" he asked.

Tori gulped down more of the black liquor. "I don't know what's real anymore. I don't even know if it matters. Maybe I did die already. Maybe I'm in Hell. God, it sure feels like it. All I know is, whatever I did in my life to hurt other people, I sure as fuck have paid in full, don't you think?"

The oily man pulled his knees up to his chest and took a long drink. "That's not for me to say."

Tori took another pull from the bottle, and the liquor tasted like sour bile. She spat it onto the concrete, the rivulets gathered into an ink-black pool and soon braided together to form some gelatinous glob.

She turned to face the oily man. Instead, she saw her father, dressed in shorts, his mayonnaise-colored belly bare, his swollen feet overflowing from a pair of flipflops. He held the bottle of clear liquid now and took a slug from it.

"Hey, Pumpkin! I heard you weren't doing so hot, so I wanted to come by and cheer you up."

Tori scrambled backward like a frightened crab. Dad's smile grew broader and brighter. He took another drink and said, "That's no way to treat your old man. Didn't you miss me?"

Her throat cracked. The inside of her mouth tasted like blood, and fear shook her when she thought about what might have been in the bottle she drank from.

"Get out of here," she croaked. "You don't belong here. You're dead."

Dad chuckled. "Dead? Where on earth did you hear that? I'm sitting right in front of you, aren't I?"

Tears dripped from her chin. She stood up, her cheeks expanding and contracting, and clutched the vessel so hard, she thought it might break in her hand. Dad hefted himself up. He looked even more bloated and yellow than she'd ever remembered seeing him. A puffed, gray hand rested on her shoulder.

"I know you and I haven't always seen eye to eye, Pumpkin, but there's one thing we can both agree on. You're a lousy sack of shit, and it's time for you to finally die."

His face contorted into a manic grin. Tori felt all the air leave her body, and she threw the bottle to the ground. It exploded in a spray of jagged glass. The black liquid showered the ground. It collected itself into a single, writhing entity that climbed its way up her leg and held her fast to the spot.

"Tsk, tsk, tsk. Honey. Is that any way to act? Now look what you've done. Didn't Daddy teach you better than to waste perfectly good alcohol? Let's get this in your tummy, where it belongs."

The rope of goo worked its way, sticky and gluey, up her body until it reached her mouth. It reared back and struck at her. She pulled her head away, but the goop pursued her until it slid down her throat and swam in her guts. It hit her like a cannonball, and she staggered onto her back. Her vision blurred as she made contact with the pavement.

Dad sat next to her and pulled her into his lap. Her back cracked as he forced her onto his body. He swaddled her like an infant and put the container of clear liquid to her lips.

"Come on, sweetheart. Time to take your medicine. I know, you don't like the taste, but we're all getting tired of your bullshit, so let's swallow it down like a good girl. That's it. Drink it all."

The fluid glugged in the bottle as she gulped, sending bubbles back in with every pull. It tasted bitter, almost like sucking on a dry aspirin. She wanted to spit it out and tried to resist the liquid pouring down her throat, but she couldn't wrench herself away. Her father kept a grip on her and forced the bottle tight against her mouth. Tori's head swam.

"Empty. Good girl! How do you feel?"

Tori spat liquid she held in her mouth right into the man's face. He frowned like a petulant child.

"That was not very nice, Victoria. Not nice at all. I think I'm going to have to punish you for that."

She could barely sit up straight and flopped back onto the chilled walkway. Her father towered over her, his face distorted and misshapen from the angle and perspective. He looked like a funhouse mirror reflection of himself. A knee jerked back and a foot ricocheted ahead. Toenails, overgrown and yellowed, jabbed into her ribs as the flipflopped foot made contact. Air puffed from her diaphragm, and she rolled into the fetal position in a vain attempt at protecting herself. More blows followed. A fist connected with her shoulders as she tucked her head into her arms. Another foot stomped down onto her leg. The flesh twisted beneath it, and Tori heard herself cry out. Breath ragged, she whimpered. Dad collapsed upon her and smashed the entirety of his weight against her, crushing her to the pavement. The pressure squeezed her guts until dizziness overcame her and darkness enveloped her.

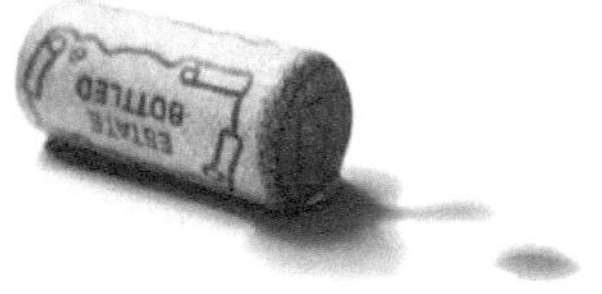

Chris Silver lay in bed, stomach twisted and sour. Even on good days, it was this way. It wasn't a good day, and it hadn't even started. He hadn't felt the urge to drink in years, but it was getting to him today. Just one wouldn't hurt. Just one. It was a lie he told himself from time to time. He'd never actually succumbed to it, but there was an itch beneath his skin this morning, and he hoped he could find other ways to scratch it.

He swung his feet over the edge of the bed and felt the soft plush of the carpet. He padded to the bathroom and took care of his most pressing concern. Having shaken the dew off the lily, he creaked and groaned out of the bedroom and down the hallway. He tiptoed past Emmy's room. Chris couldn't bring himself to think of it as anyone else's room. His last day on earth, that would be Emmy's room. Five years after she died, he'd forced himself to put the crib and the dresser out by the road for the garbage man. That was thirty years ago, and he still hated himself for that. The walls were the same soft rose-pink Margaret had chosen. Chris had picked up the paint days after they brought Emmy Viola home from the hospital. He knew the room needed to be updated and repainted. The carpet was as old as the house. But where was he going? He'd be dead in a few years, probably, and décor would be someone else's problem. It was Emmy's room. It would always be Emmy's room.

Yet, someone had taken her room, and he felt a twinge of guilt for that. He imagined that if Emmy had lived, she would've shared. He'd invented the grown-up version of Emmy in his head. She was petite with the same strawberry blonde curls, only styled more maturely. Grown-up Emmy was generous and polite with only a hint of her father's self-righteousness, just enough to be endearing instead of obnoxious. Grown-up Emmy would've gladly given her room to a woman in desperate need of help, he decided. The pang of guilt eased but didn't die completely. It never went away.

He filled the coffee carafe with enough water to make a couple of cups for himself and his guest, popped in a filter, and scooped out two tablespoons of ground coffee. The rich aroma invigorated him. He hoped the smell would perk his guest, and they might attend an AA meeting together. He needed to go to one himself. The stress of having a drinker in his home was getting under his skin.

Still, he understood she'd been through a lot. Sleep might be what she needed. He would be as quiet as possible until she emerged.

The coffeemaker gurgled and hissed. Steam lifted up as the deep brown liquid dripped into the carafe. He moved to the living room and flipped on the television. Channel six offered an infomercial for a salad tosser. Chris flipped past the early morning news broadcast to a 90s sitcom with a bad laugh track. He couldn't handle the news. For the first thirty years of his life, he'd watched the news religiously, but stories of death and destruction and the awful things people do to each other depressed him so much, he had to stop. Now, any time he saw the vacuous, empty, emotionless faces of news broadcasters, he flipped to another station. He knew more than anyone what humans were capable of.

He watched the characters of the sitcom get into a variety of stupid misunderstandings that even the most nitwitted person could avoid in real life. The coffeemaker beeped, and he shuffled to the kitchen. The floor was cold against his feet. He checked the thermostat on the way and bumped it up to seventy. The burner groaned and hummed and, before long, heat came down from the vents.

He poured himself a cup of coffee, black. The thought of watching the boring misadventures of a bunch of thirty-something folks held little appeal for him. He took a steaming-hot first sip, that sip that hits the bloodstream and jumpstarts the heart. He walked to the French doors that led to his greening, moss-coated back porch. Vines and brown grass waved in the brittle breeze. The swing set rusted like a shipyard hulk in the twisting brambles.

A single swing rocked back and forth. The movement drew him closer to the door. Before he realized what he was doing, he'd turned the lock and threw open doors. The cold rippled through his thin, striped pajamas. He could see her, staring out from behind a curtain of curls. Her stare was wistful. She didn't appear to be pained or sad or even happy. She just offered up a vision of what might've been but wasn't. Couldn't be.

Grief squeezed him like a vice. It wasn't the first time he'd seen her out there, playing with her toys—decades-old relics that would never bring joy to anyone. His breath hitched, and he doubled over, the mental pain jabbing like a thousand daggers. Could she see him? Did she remember dying? Was she trapped? Did she feel pain when she died?

The last question haunted him each and every day. He visualized the semi smashing into the back of the car, the panels crumpling, his child screaming and crying as the metal twisted into her body, ripping the life out of her. And Margaret. His college sweetheart. She'd be forever fresh-faced and freckled with skin as smooth as silk. Her body would never sag with age. They'd missed the chance to grow old together, to learn to love the little imperfections that came along as death neared. Wrinkles and the silver strands that wound their way through thinning hair. The aches and cracks that came with getting out of bed in the morning. He'd never had the chance to truly love her unconditionally. And the void left by her absence was a chasm he'd never be able to fill.

He recalled the last time he saw Emmy out there. He wasn't even sure he'd really seen her at first. She peeked out from behind a lilac bush, curious but cautious like a rabbit. He'd been cooking a meal long since forgotten and set the pan in the sink. A mist waved back and forth in the dim evening, and he didn't give it much thought until he turned. There was a face. *Her* face. It forced all the breath out of him, and he crashed through the back door, ripped down the stairs, and raced toward her. He wanted to grab her and swing her through the air and hold her to him and smell her sweet, soft hair and kiss her plump baby cheeks. But as soon as he reached her, she was gone, and he was broken anew.

Chris resisted the urge now to rush out and scoop her up and beg her to stay. She hadn't visited often over the years, but she did seem to show up when he was low and thinking about drinking. Or about joining her. He'd never told anyone about the nights he lay in bed, salt from his tears stinging his face, considering a razor blade in the bathtub or a cocktail of pills and booze. Comics always pulled him back from the brink. The idea that everyday people could do extraordinary things and save the day gave him hope.

QuickSilver was a joke at first. A funny idea that he, a paunchy goofball, could be a superhero. It was a way to escape, so he started creating stories in his mind about QuickSilver's adventures. Those stories took on a life of their own, and before long, he couldn't control it anymore. It became bigger than he was, so he stopped fighting it. And he had helped people. If that was his fate, who was he to question it—or try to stop it?

Emmy's form faded and disappeared completely. Dejected, he moved back inside. His chilled skin felt numb against the heat from his kitchen. He clutched his coffee cup and drank deeply. It wasn't enough, though. He set the mug back down and threw open the cabinets one by one, finally searching beneath the sink. He rushed to the hallway bathroom and pulled open the cabinet under that sink. Listerine would taste awful, but that's all he had. Scope would've been better. He twisted the white cap and held it under his nose. It smelled like some facsimile of mint mixed with medicine and chemicals. Chris set it down and put his hands against the countertop, breathing deeply. The bandage that covered most of his face alarmed him when he caught a glimpse of it in the mirror. He looked like a ghastly version of himself, a person he didn't even recognize. He needed a meeting. Going now would be better than sucking down the antiseptic, foul-tasting mouthwash just for the alcohol. If he was that desperate, it was time to get help.

Chris put the cap back on the mouthwash and marched to Emmy's old room. He knocked lightly and listened at the crack. He tried a little louder but still heard nothing, so he turned the knob and eased himself inside. The room was empty. The air mattress had been slept on, but there was no sign of Tori.

The surge of adrenaline started, and he ran out the front door. Someone was in trouble. Someone needed QuickSilver.

CHAPTER 19

Orange daylight poured over her face, and Tori groaned. She expected to roll over and find her dad snoring next to her, but he was nowhere to be found. It was more of a relief than she expected. Her ribs ached, and she tasted blood. *Something* had beaten the shit out of her, there was no doubt about that. She sat unsteadily and studied herself. Purple, thumb-shaped ovals were already forming in the meaty part of her arms. She rolled her jeans up and saw bloodied welts slashing up her shins. Thick, brown-red scabs formed on her knees where she'd fallen on the craggy asphalt.

Someone shuffled along on the walkway. Keys jangled. Tori eased herself up and stood. Her knees buckled under the strain, but she fought to keep herself up. Her legs quaked and her elbow shook.

"Lady, we don't open for another hour. If you don't leave, I'm going to have to call the cops."

It was the same man who'd sold her beer the day before; he was wearing the same flannel shirt and dirty jeans.

Tori coughed, and something that tasted subterranean chunked into her mouth. She swallowed it back down.

"I think I'm hurt," she said.

Mr. Flannel was halfway inside the store, and he already had his phone out. The cowbell clanged.

"All right, fine," Tori huffed. "That's some downhome motherfucking hospitality right there. I'll go die in the street."

Her body ached as she hobbled, determined to keep putting one foot after the other until she reached the rough asphalt. A hissing caught her off guard, and she expected to see the wriggling mass of appendages that marched her down there the night before. She smelled like urine, and it took her a few seconds to realize she'd pissed all over herself. The memory of the oozing black goo she'd drank disgusted her so much, she put her hands to her knees and stopped walking. She felt like she might puke, but she choked it back down. She wondered what it was. She also wondered about the clear liquor her father—no, it wasn't her father; it was some mental construct intended to rip her insides out—poured down her gullet. Whatever she'd consumed, it wasn't enough, and the urge to drink again seized her.

That's right. Drink some more. It's about time we ended this, don't you think? Haven't you hit rock bottom yet? You did just spend the night on the concrete in front of a convenience store. Oh, but how you've fallen. Can you see that? Or are you too far gone?

It wasn't lost on Tori. She knew how far she'd fallen, only it didn't matter anymore. She'd tried to fight it, but it overpowered her. Did she have any fight at all left in her?

Her legs ached. Her feet felt like hamburger. The road was still raw against her exposed feet. She limped. Her purse would be back at Chris's house, and if she could just get back there, she might be able to walk back and get more beer. Or maybe she could convince Chris to let her borrow his car so she could go to Harrington's to get what she really wanted. Maybe vodka. Maybe more gin. Beer had never been her drink, but it would do if she had no other choice.

She made the turn onto Chris's street. A car raced toward her, and she staggered into dry, fragile bushes. The branches cut into her skin. The car screeched to a halt. Chris jumped out and ran over to her.

"Where have you been?" His voice was agitated and accusatory. It almost made her laugh, but she let the question hang in the air long enough that it made her irrationally angry.

"I don't have to tell you where I've been," she spat. Tori would be hard-pressed to explain it. She wasn't certain she understood it herself.

Chris's face puffed and turned crimson.

"Do you want to die?" he screamed.

Tori tried to walk around him. If she could just get back to his house, she could get her purse. Her most pressing need had nothing to do with the man in front of her.

"Quiet, I'm trying to get something to drink," she said.

He stepped in front of her and crossed his arms over his chest. It was the same action he'd taken to scare off the boys who chased her all those years ago. She wanted his help. She wanted him to save her. But that thirst demanded to be quenched, that gaping maw had opened up again, and it was like trying to deny herself oxygen. Right now, she felt like she had been holding her breath.

"Listen to me." His words echoed out over the otherwise-still neighborhood as the sun crested the horizon and illuminated the birds that nested beyond the reeds. "If you don't stop, you are going to die. I can't let that happen. I'm all you've got right now. Why won't you even try?"

Hot rage flared in her chest, and the urge to leap at him and attack built up so strong, her fingers clenched into fists.

You don't have to take this shit. Just take him out and get what you need.

"No." She said the word out loud, even though she hadn't intended to.

"No?" he yelled. "No? You can't give up. I won't let you."

Her muscles twitched and contracted. The back of her neck felt sweaty. She resisted the instinct to attack. She turned and walked back toward the convenience store. The alternative would be leaping at him and ripping him to shreds. The piece of her that could resist knew that would destroy everything. She didn't want to hurt anyone, let alone end someone's life. Tori had already done that, and it cut away at her insides. She couldn't do it again.

He followed her, unwilling or unable to back off and leave her alone.

"I won't let you do this, Victoria," he called. His breath wheezed out of him as he jogged to keep up.

"You don't understand, Chris," she told him. "This isn't for my safety. It's for yours. Turn around and go home."

"And watch you self-destruct? Come with me to a meeting. Get some help. I'll even take you to detox if that's what it takes. I'll be by your side the whole way."

He's not backing down. You need to get rid of him. What you need right now is another drink.

Heat rippled over her numb, chilled flesh. It felt like a furnace had sprung to life and scorched her. Anger gripped her, but somewhere deep inside, she knew it wasn't her own anger. She understood that the *thing* had taken control again. She understood, but could she stop it? Her fingernails dug into the flesh of her palms. Blood puddled into the crescent-shaped wounds.

She stomped down the road, hoping the distance would keep her from doing something she would regret. Flashbacks of smashing that bottle over Amelia's head flitted into her mind and played back like a bad horror movie.

He shouted, but she could barely make out the words. She felt like she was being pulled in two different directions. Her feet dashed against the asphalt. She stumbled, catching herself. Something thrashed furiously within her.

Breath seethed through her teeth, and she turned to face Chris, who had his arms still folded defiantly over his chest. Her bare, bloodied feet slapped the road as she ran at him, fists flailing. Animal growls roared from her insides as she assailed him, batting at his shoulders and chest. He clutched her wrists and pushed her backward.

Tori put her hands to her knees and caught her breath. He stared at her with a mix of determination and heartbreak. He cared. She saw in him someone who actually gave a damn, genuinely and completely. She saw in him a savior. But the black, twisting entity that had taken up residence in her wanted him dead. It raged inside her.

Tori took a few steps back toward the marsh by the roadside. Her feet brushed against the muddy bank. The closer she got to it, the more the beast lurched within her. It was the same experience near the ocean, the same experience in the bathtub, the same experience every time she'd come near water. Even in the hospital, it battled as her body was flooded by water in an effort to revive her.

Tori dashed into the ice-cold quagmire. Shock overcame her as her naked feet clutched at the slimy muck.

"Fight me," she screamed. Her hair clung to her face as sweat poured down. The frigid water battled against the overwhelming heat that radiated from within her.

Chris hesitated at the bankside. He folded the legs of his jeans up to reveal pale, blue-veined legs. He waded in, arms pumping in front of him in an effort to keep his balance. He clutched her elbow and pulled.

"Knock this off," he growled. "Get out of this water right now. You're going to freeze out here. Get in the car. You need help.'

Her blood boiled. The entity clawed at her insides, and Tori jerked her elbow away from him. She reared back and punched him in the face, an action that horrified her. It was out of her control. She turned away from him, unable to watch; she couldn't bear to see if she'd hurt him. There was a sound, a liquid gurgle. Tori waded farther into the slippery depths.

Chris reached out again, and blind fury overcame her. She clutched his extended arm and pulled him toward her. His eyes widened in terror as he tried to snatch his arm back, but it was too late. She was upon him, smashing his face with her fist. Chris's body stumbled, and he splashed into the water. Tori squeezed his neck and pushed his head into the brackish drink. His pulse thudded rapidly as he struggled against her. Bubbles surfaced as he thrashed around. Her hand tightened its grip around his slippery throat. The skin under his chin turned blue as she held him steady. His body continued to fight, but his movements slowed, his fight weakened. The pulse at the side of his neck slowed.

Her grip loosened. She didn't want to do this. He was dying. The memory of the girl she'd killed flashed in blood-red detail in her face. The teenager's face lay dashed against the asphalt, a spray of glass surrounding her, and the same gut-rending fear wrapped itself around her.

Water swirled and churned as he tried to push himself up out of the water. The thing that had taken up residence inside her wouldn't let her help him. She cupped her hands, desperate to rid herself of this horrible inhabitant, and gulped down salty, slimy fluid. Tori grimaced at the awful taste. She fought the urge to spit it all back out, clutched up another handful, and drank it down. The water bubbled up in her belly, churning like a stormy sea. But the entity was not leaving. She chugged more of the filthy, mucky fluid, desperate to evict it from her body. She panted. Nausea overcame her. The churning grew stronger inside her. It knocked her backward into the marsh. She struggled her way back up and fell back to her knees. Something slid its way up from her belly and into her throat, and Tori instinctively opened her mouth and felt around for it. A sharp fang bit down on her forefinger. She recoiled then felt herself choking. Her face felt hot. A long object slithered from her mouth, followed by dozens more. They were all stark white and swam off into the water. Tori held out a hand and caught the last snake as it dropped. It tried to wiggle away, but she studied it and turned the white creature to face her. She dropped it into the water with a *plunk* once she saw it had no eyes.

Chris Silver floated motionless before her, and her heart lodged itself in her throat. There was no resistance this time. Nothing held her back from clutching him by the chest and pulling him toward the roadway. She felt freer than she had in a long, long time.

Hazy, gray water bubbled up from Chris's sinuses. His body went limp and his lungs burned, pleading for air. Something hooked into his armpits and hefted him out of the marsh. Ice spread from his core to his extremities, and he shivered in a whole-body convulsion. Evergreens blurred like a Monet painting. The sensation of floating transformed and he felt rough gravel beneath his back. Someone leaned over him, but he couldn't make out the person's features. The silence mystified him so much he wondered if he was still alive.

Fluid rippled up in his belly and gushed out onto the asphalt. He inhaled a flood of air. Dizziness overcame him, and he retched again. Chris felt something long and smooth slide down his throat, and he gagged and tried to pull it back up. Instead, it settled into his belly.

His eyes focused, and Tori's face hovered over his. Her voice was insistent, but it sounded dim, as if she was speaking from another room in a house.

"Hum hon, Hiss. Hugh aff oo ache hup. Ache hup. Mum hon. Ache hup."

Befuddled, he tried to ask her what she was talking about, but his throat burned. A slap stung his cheek, and he jerked upright. He crab-walked away from her. Her hands waved back and forth.

"No, no, no," she shouted. "Please. I'm sorry. I swear, I won't hurt you."

He could hear her now; her voice was strained and gravelly. Chris coughed, and something squirmed. He coughed again in the hopes of bringing it up, but it wouldn't move beyond the back of his throat.

She knelt by his side and put an arm around him.

"Are you okay?" she asked.

"What happened to you?" he choked out, a wave of tears flowing out along with the words.

Her body shook against his. "I don't know. I don't know what happened to me. Something had a hold over me. But it's over now. I can't explain it, but it's gone."

"Then you'll get help?"

She nodded, her soaked hair splattering him with tiny droplets of marsh water.

"Do you need to go to the hospital?" she asked.

Chris assessed himself. His breathing seemed normal, if a bit shallow. He could see clearly and hear well. The bandage that had been covering his face must've been left behind in the swamp. He decided he'd be all right and shook his head. Tori extended her arms, and he grasped her hands. She tugged as hard as she could to help him up, staggering back in the process. On his feet, he felt unstable and weak.

"Let's just get you back to the car. I'll drive you home," she said. "You need to get out of these wet clothes and warmed up."

Tori tucked an arm around his shoulders. Her fingertips barely reached the expanse of his back, and she strained to prop him up and walk him back to the abandoned Subaru just down the road.

Chris could hear the *ding-ding-ding-ding* of the open-door alarm going off. Each step sent excruciating bolts of pain down his back. The pain he felt the most was inside. His insides felt far worse. His pride was shattered. It was the same shame he'd felt when that nasty thug slashed his face. He could've protected that woman, but he'd been bested. That kind of disappointment hovered over him like a phantom, and he found himself bested again. He'd tried to save someone. It nearly cost him his life, but he didn't know how to stop. Could he keep from turning in to QuickSilver, even if he wanted to?

Chris's back popped when Tori eased him into the passenger's seat. She crossed in front of the car to the driver's side and sat, adjusted the seat, and closed the door. The silent ride home only took a minute, but it seemed like an hour of emptiness neither of them could fill. His mouth hung open stupidly, and his cheeks burned with the embarrassment of his antics. Chris couldn't stop shaking. The vent spewed still-cold air at him, but by the time they reached the driveway, it had warmed slightly. He frowned when she turned off the ignition.

Tori helped him out of the car and into the house and waited outside his bedroom door when he went in to clean himself. The tiny bathroom off his bedroom wasn't big enough for more than one person to turn around. He slipped out of his soggy, frozen clothes and wrapped his chilled flesh against the thin, scratchy fabric of a towel. The shivering subsided, and he moved to the dresser and selected a pair of clean jeans, a thick Son of Satan hoodie, boxers, and a pair of wool socks.

Once he was decent and warm, he walked out to see Tori, still shaking, hair dripping onto the carpet. Her puffed, darkened eyes looked doleful as she stared at the floor. He didn't fully trust her, but her expression revealed remorse, empathy, and compassion––things he hadn't noticed in her before.

"Go on and get yourself cleaned up," he said.

A low rumble of a laugh built in her chest. "I want to," she said. "I hope I can."

"No, I mean literally. Go change out of those clothes. Amelia left your stuff in the living room."

"But are you ..."

"I'm okay," he said. "You get yourself back up to room temperature, and you and I will go find a meeting."

Tori's shoulders shook. She slumped to her knees, water from her hair dripping onto the hallway carpet. Her body curled into itself as she sobbed. The familiar rush of adrenaline hit him like a bullet. He dropped to his knees and put a hand on her back. A flood of memories from the short time he had as Emmy's father overwhelmed him, and tears gathered in his eyes.

"It's going to be okay," he whispered. "I'm here to help you.

I've been where you are."

She looked up at him, snot rolling down her mouth, face red, mouth agape. Tori struggled to catch her breath.

"You ... you've ... you've never killed anyone."

The words stung him. He always believed he could've saved Margaret and Emmy. If he'd been a gentleman and drove them to the grocery store instead of sulking at home, reading and avoiding human interaction at any cost. At the cost of their lives. Maybe if he'd been driving, it would've been different somehow. He couldn't rationalize the *how* exactly.

"I could've saved my family," he said, gulping down a saltwater lump. "I know what it feels like to lose everything."

Tori wiped her face with the sleeve of her sweater. She listened. Really listened.

"My little girl loved the grocery store. She was the happiest kid you've ever seen. Always smiling. Riding in the cart was like a day at Disneyland. And I was a miserable asshole," he told her. "Back then, being around other people was ... well, it was just hard for me. Shopping seemed like a stupid chore. The only thing that made it even bearable was Emmy. She had this joie de vivre. Never fussed. Most little kids her age screamed bloody murder. Sometimes, I'd push the cart and run really fast, and she would just cackle with delight."

He was smiling and crying at the same time. Tori stared, waiting.

"Anyway, the day it happened, I was in one of my moods. I just couldn't be bothered. Emmy begged me to go and push her, but I brushed her off. So, Margaret gathered her up and headed off. They were gone a really long time, and after a while, I got worried. Before I could even go out to look for them, a cop pulled up in my driveway and told me what happened. A distracted trucker didn't see Margaret put on her brakes, and the truck barreled right into them. Emmy didn't stand a chance in the backseat. Margaret lived a little longer. She made it to the hospital, but I didn't even get to say goodbye. She was gone by the time I got there."

Tori sat up and Chris sat across from her. She held his bitter-cold hands in her own.

"I'm so sorry," she said.

Chris wanted to tell her about QuickSilver, but he couldn't bring himself to reveal his secret identity. His mouth snapped shut again.

"I used to be somebody," she started, her face contorted into a half-smile. "Then I accidentally hit a kid with my car. She died. And I couldn't stop replaying it in my head. That's when I started drinking. For a while, it worked. Then, it seemed like the more I drank, the worse it got. By then, I couldn't stop."

He nodded. It was so much like his own story. The moment was disrupted by a peculiar feeling that nestled itself inside him. The object he couldn't quite dislodge from his throat unsettled him, and he pressed his fingers against his throat. Probably some slime or sediment. His nostrils still burned from inhaling the brine.

Tori grunted as she stood. Chris followed her.

"Do you think you might be ready to get help?" he asked. The compulsion to drink overwhelmed him, and he realized going to AA was just as necessary for him as it was for her.

She slid a sweater-covered hand over her face, wiping away the tears.

"Yeah. That's a good idea. Let me just get myself together," she said.

Something occurred to Chris as a droplet from her hair settled on his hand as she walked off in search of warm, dry clothes. It was back in 1983. A sun-lit day when the shop was still out on Beach.

Emmy and Margaret had been two years gone already.

It was the kind of day that made him feel like it might be okay. Sun glinted off the ocean across the street. He hadn't completely fallen into despair by then. He drank, but not all the time. He worked all day long in an effort to be somewhere other than home.

A little girl in a bikini, barefoot and racing for her life and a couple of stupid kids trailing her, zipped down the sidewalk, their feet slapping the concrete all the way. He'd been standing by the window, watching people flit about, eating hot dogs and playing Frisbee when she blurred by. She wasn't the first girl he'd seen them harassing. The sniveling shits had been unsupervised for days, hanging out under the pilings of the gazebo, shouting obscenities to people, mostly girls and young women. He'd stomped to the door, sick to death of this behavior. The boys scrambled toward his store. He'd stepped outside and QuickSilver kicked in. He'd crossed his arms over his chest, lowered his voice a couple of octaves, and they clattered to a stop just before crashing into him. Like most cowardly turds, they darted off before he could get the police involved. The girl stood shivering behind him, her eyes filled with terror. He'd introduced himself. And she'd introduced herself. Tori. Tori Garrett. When she'd told him before, he couldn't remember, not clearly anyway. But he knew now, without a doubt.

They'd walked across the street to the beach together. He'd seen her parents, distant from each other. Her father had been splayed out in a beach chair, crushed cans littering the sand. The look she'd given him was one of fear as she scampered off. It was the fear that he would judge her. She was just a little kid. And it occurred to him. He *had* judged her. He'd judged the grown-up version of her for the things he'd done himself, hadn't he?

He'd asked her to come in for *Wonder Woman* number three-hundred. She never came in to get it. Chris pulled down the attic ladder and walked up. They'd go to a meeting soon. First, there was something he had to do.

CHAPTER 20

Tori wrapped her hair into a towel turban. She hiked up her jeans, which gapped at the waist.

"Hmm. Must've lost a few pounds," she said to herself.

It felt good to be dry. It felt good to be free. The voice had left her, and she heard her own thoughts for the first time in a long time. That was scary enough. Her own thoughts told her to go get a drink. That incessant quiver worked its way down her arm again. She knew she had a long way to go, but she was ready to take the first steps.

She wasn't entirely sure she was ready to leave Cape May though, and she envisioned a future living there. Going back to Montclair churned her stomach. The thought of picking up where she left off—if that was even possible—seemed like a huge step backwards. Cape May still offered a fresh slate. She'd just have to pull herself together.

Tori unfurled her hair and shook out the remnants of the water. She looked into the bathroom mirror and saw someone who had hit rock bottom. Her face was drawn and haggard. Lines framed the sides of her mouth. Shit, she thought. It doesn't get more rock bottom than waking up on the concrete, shitfaced and desperate. She shook her head at the memory. She wondered if she'd ever be able to forget, and then it occurred to her that she never wanted to forget. She needed to hold onto that memory so she'd never slide back there.

Something clunked just outside the bathroom door, and Chris called out, "Hey, when you're done, I'll be in the car."

She turned on the faucet and splashed cold water on her face. The absence of nausea, the peace in her head, overwhelmed her and tears slid down her face. She smiled at her reflection.

"Damn, you need to get a grip, woman," she told the image staring back at her.

She gave herself a once-over and opened the bathroom door. It was time to take charge. She took a long walk down the hallway and out the front door.

The Subaru idled, and Chris ducked down in the car for a second before reemerging. She got in. The heater seared her skin. She was starting to feel human again.

Chris stared straight ahead throughout the ride to Rio Grande. His stoic silence unnerved her, especially after the way he poured his heart out to her in the hallway.

The sight of the Rio Grande Unitarian Universalist Fellowship stabbed her heart. Yes, Bracken was an asshole, but it was the first time she'd felt anything for a man in a long time. The thought that she'd been betrayed scorched her still, and she wondered if she'd ever let anyone get close to her again. Maybe being alone was the best thing now. How could she even think about getting involved with someone until she could pull her shit together and get clean?

Chris parked and dug around in the back seat for something. He jerked upright and said, "Oh, you can go on ahead. I'll catch up with you. I just have to grab something."

Tori got out of the car and made her way to the metal double doors. She held back and waited. Chris rounded the corner with a brown paper sack tucked under his armpit. The doors *clanked* when she pushed through them. She held the door for him, and they descended the stairs together. The place smelled like cigarettes and casseroles.

A few people sat in folding chairs when they entered. The same guy she'd seen in the sweater vest the last time she'd tried this now set a plate of sugar cookies on a long table.

"Welcome," he said with a broad smile. "We'll be getting started in just a few minutes. Are you new?"

Chris cleared his throat. "She is. I've been here a few times."

"Great! Well, we're glad to have you."

Tori's stomach ached. The thought of sitting up front, exposed and absolutely anything *but* anonymous, froze her.

"We can sit in the back, if you'd be more comfortable," Chris whispered.

He led her by the arm to seats in the last row on the far left so they could make a quick exit if she needed a moment. The gesture comforted her. A few other people entered, the metal doors slamming behind them. Each slam made her jump.

The man with the cookies jogged up to the podium.

"All right, folks. Might as well get started. My name is Alex, and I'm an alcoholic. If you want, you can stand up and introduce yourself."

A woman in an oversized chambray shirt and a pair of ripped jeans stood up and said, "My name is Jane, and I'm an alcoholic. I've been sober for twenty-seven days. I began drinking when I was eleven and snuck liquor out of my parents' cabinet. By the time I got into college, I was drinking every single day. I'm trying to stay sober because I found out a couple of months ago that I'm having a baby next spring. My doctor says I have a good chance of having a healthy baby, if I can just stay on this path."

A spattering of applause followed, Jane sat down, and a burly man in a car coat stood up.

"Hey, my name is Stephen, and I'm an alcoholic. I've been sober for almost ten years. I started drinking because I lost my job during the recession back in '08, and I just couldn't get it together financially. We lost the house, and my wife left not long after that. It all kind of fell apart. And then I fell apart."

Heads nodded. Tori found herself nodding along, too. Stephen shuffled his feet and stuffed his hands in his pockets before he sat again.

More applause rang out. It went on like this across the room like some sort of exposed confessional. The meeting leader was there to absolve them all and forgive them for their sins. Fear rattled Tori, and she didn't know if she'd be able to stand up and confess when her turn arrived.

The stink of smoke caught her attention, and she jerked her head toward the window. A man with stringy, gray hair sat by the open window, frigid air blowing in, puffing a cigarette. No one else seemed to mind or even notice. Tori looked at the faces in the room, really studied them. Not one person looked happy. Most of them looked absolutely miserable. She looked next to her and saw Chris; he shivered slightly and wore the look of a man who wished he could be just about anywhere else. He probably would've had a better time at an Ankara prison.

A puddle of sweat gathered in her philtrum. She licked her lips and tasted the salt. The air coming in from the window chilled the sweat to her face, and she sucked in a deep breath. It eased some of her nausea. Her head still throbbed, and her hands jittered.

Chris stood beside her and said, "Hi, I'm Chris. I've been sober for twenty-one years and seven months."

More applause. It pounded in her head like a mallet chipping away at her resolve. Her palms sweated.

Chris slipped a warm, dry hand into hers and nodded at her. She stood up. Her knees felt wobbly.

"Hi," she said. Her voice cracked. "My name is Victoria. I'm an alcoholic. I need help."

The room was silent for a moment as her words settled. The applause built up. She sat and exhaled. The act of getting the words out freed her more than she believed it would.

Chris looked at her and smiled. He put his hand back into hers and squeezed it. She felt more at ease.

Chairs screeched as someone got up and poured a cup of coffee. The cigarette-smoking guy returned to his seat, reeking of tar and nicotine.

Alex droned at the podium about choices. No one in the room seemed to be listening. The smoker sauntered back to the window, shoved it open, and lit another cigarette. Some of the platitudes were trite and obvious, but it occurred to her that if it was all really obvious, she probably wouldn't be sitting there, wishing she could suck down the hand sanitizer in her purse.

She crossed her legs and her foot twitched up and down. She sat on her hands, which would not stop shaking.

"Does anyone have a success story they'd like to share with the group today?" Alex asked.

Stephen stood up.

"Some friends invited me out the other night. Everyone around me was drinking, but I just had soda. It's the first time I've gone to a gathering where I knew there'd be alcohol in years. I wasn't tempted."

More applause. It slammed her head. Would they just stop clapping already? She knew that sounded bitchy, but every little thing irritated her, and she couldn't understand why. Stephen had every reason to be applauded. She pulled her hands out from under her and put her head in them. She hadn't recalled a headache that rattled her so much. Her eyesight blurred from the pain. Nausea bubbled up, and she instinctively darted for the door in search of the bathroom. A chair screeched behind her, but she couldn't turn around. She stumbled up the stairs and into a foyer where she spotted the restrooms. She slammed her way into one of them, unsure that it was even the ladies' room. Vomit spewed forth just as she reached the first stall. It was all yellow bile, and another torrent followed along, this one tinged with red.

The sight of blood startled her, and she hugged the toilet. Sweat clung to her hair, and it felt like the fires of Hell itself were steaming up from her sweater.

She clutched the sides of the toilet and pushed herself up. Her stomach burned.

"Tori? Are you okay?" A muffled voice called from the other side of the bathroom door. She wiped her nose with the back of her hand and turned to the sink. The automatic faucet came on, and she ran her trembling hands underneath it, gathering pools into her palms. The simple act of splashing her face felt like a spa day.

She gathered up more water, slurped some in her mouth, swished it around, and spat. Slightly revived, she walked out.

Chris leaned against the wall next to the door, and he snapped to attention as soon as she opened it.

"Are you okay?" he asked.

"I think I'll be okay. It's like the worst case of the flu I've ever had."

"It's withdrawal," he replied. "Not fun at all. I know. I hallucinated for days when I quit drinking. Couldn't leave my bed. I was constantly seeing ... well, I saw people in my house who couldn't have been there. It's like living in a nightmare."

She stared at him, aghast.

"I guess I'm not coming off as supportive, but I don't want to give you the false sense of security that this is going to be an easy thing," he said.

The headache was thundering again, and her ears felt like they were clogged.

"Come on," he said, hooking her elbow with his forearm. "I'll take you home. You could probably use something to eat, maybe some coffee. I make the best damned omelets you've ever had."

The idea of eating churned her stomach, but she didn't resist. Food had been the last thing on her mind for weeks, and it might ease the pounding in her skull.

He helped her into the car and closed the door for her. The paper bag was still tucked under his arm, and she wondered what he could be carting around as he crossed in front of the car and opened the driver's side door.

Chris sat down and the car shook under his weight. The paper sack rattled as he rifled through it. He tucked something into his lap and said, "I'm proud of you for doing this. And years ago, I told you to come in and get a copy of *Wonder Woman*. Do you remember?"

Tori's mouth dropped open. She remembered. The memory of that day had stayed with her for decades. It comforted her during the rockiest of days when her parents screamed and slammed doors. It gave her a standard for men when her father walked out and didn't return for days at a time. It opened a curtain onto the kind of man fathers could be. She'd never have one like Chris, but it was enough to educate her on the wrongness of her family life. Chris made her feel safe.

Even sitting in his car, a headache ripping into her skull and a puddle of sweat gathering in her clothes, she felt like he could save her. He slid a comic book into her lap. Wonder Woman stood atop the Invisible Plane. Batman, Superman, and Hawkman—there were others, but those were the only three she could recall by sight—surged ahead in midair to help Wonder Woman save the day.

She stared at the Mylar-bagged, thirty-five-year-old comic. It was a special anniversary issue at that.

"I can't accept this," she said, pushing it back toward him. "It's got to be worth quite a bit."

Chris shrugged. "Nah. Not particularly. Mint condition, encapsulated, it'd probably fetch a hundred bucks tops at auction. But I want you to have it, because you *are* Wonder Woman. You've fought back at every challenge you've faced. Coming here today, taking that first step and admitting you have a problem, that takes courage. I promised you this comic all those years ago, and you should keep it."

He clutched the steering wheel and discomfort flashed across his face.

"Are you all right?" she asked.

He shuddered and said, "Yeah. Sorry. I could really use some food. Let's get out of here."

CHAPTER 21

The smell of frying eggs sent Tori bolting for the bathroom. Her head felt like someone smashed it in a car door, and her body shook as she hovered over the toilet bowl. Her stomach had already been depleted of all its contents. There was only the taste of acid left. Her muscles jerked as she dry-heaved.

Once she was certain nothing was coming up, she stood and held herself steady against the countertop. The fragrance of coffee wafted in from the kitchen, and she eased herself out of the bathroom and down the hallway toward the soothing aroma.

Chris stood over the stove, staring at the eggs in the pan as if they'd burst into flames if he didn't monitor them constantly. Tori opened up cabinets until she found the coffee mugs and took one out. She poured herself a cup of coffee and inhaled the steam coming off of it. It smelled fresh and earthy. It tasted rich and delicate with the slightest chocolatey aftertaste.

Chris flipped the omelet in the pan, and it sizzled.

"Should be ready in just a few seconds," he announced.

Tori wasn't particularly interested in food, but she'd try. Dishes clattered as he folded an omelet onto a plate. He sprinkled salt and pepper onto it and turned to face Tori. There was something not quite right about him. A fog wisped across his irises, something hazy. It chilled her blood.

Chris walked around her and put the plate on the table. She sat with her coffee cup, put it down, and lifted a fork with a shaky hand to scoop up a mouthful of omelet. The eggs tasted buttery and delicious, even if she didn't have much of an appetite for it.

After about four bites, the nausea dissipated. Her head felt more like a standard hammer was smacking her in place of a sledgehammer. Chris sat down across from her and dug into his breakfast.

"Any good?" he asked.

"Yes. Thanks. I do feel a little better."

He stuffed a large chunk of eggs into his mouth and chewed loudly. Tori scrunched her nose involuntarily and put down her fork.

"I think I've had enough," she said.

She stood and turned to see his back yard out the window. A tangle of vines wound its way around a rusted swing set. The place needed some serious landscaping.

"Do you mind if I step out onto the back porch for a few minutes? I'm sweating so much. I just need some fresh air."

Chris said, "Oh, of course," over a large chunk of half-chewed eggs.

The French doors creaked when she pulled them open. The sun was already high in the sky, but the wind whipped through the trees and rustled the leaves. A chain on the swing set clanged against a metal pole. Tori walked barefoot onto the porch, feeling the splintered, rough wood against her feet. Gooseflesh raised on her arms. The salty air swirled through her hair and dried the sweat that clung to her whole body. She should've felt refreshed, but she just felt on-edge. She couldn't shake the feeling that something bad was about to happen.

A wisp of something caught her eye over by the hedges just

beyond the swings. It was indistinct, but she could've sworn she saw a pair of eyes and the faint whorl of hair. She studied it as if it was an insect in amber. Before she could make out any features, it faded away. The prickling on her skin subsided. The fear that the nightmare of hallucinations wasn't yet over froze her to the spot for a few seconds.

Tori walked back inside, her skin now numb and cold. She shivered, but she couldn't be sure if it was the change in temperature, fear, or the constant twitching she'd had to contend with for far longer than she cared to recall.

Chris sat devoid of any expression, shoveling another forkful of eggs into his mouth. A ripple right at the fresh scar his bandage once covered held her attention.

"Something the matter?" he asked. "Did you see her, too?"

The question caught her off guard, and she didn't say anything for a moment. "Her?" she replied.

Chris scooted the chair back and took his plate to the sink. "No one," he said. She studied him as he scrubbed the dishes. A tremor, slight at first, vibrated across his shoulders. She saw the rough hairs on the back of his neck stand on end. A dish smashed against the floor, and at first, she thought he'd deliberately threw it until she noticed the tremor had worked its way down his arms. He jumped back to avoid the jumble of ceramic shards. Tori knelt and picked up the few large pieces and tossed them in the trashcan. There was a broom right next to it, so she swept up the few remaining bits so Chris wouldn't step on them. He stood, staring at the clean space where the debris had been scattered. The only movement came from the long, fish belly-colored scar that ran along his cheekbone and down to the corner of his mouth. Something beneath the flesh bulged and squirmed. Tori closed her eyes for a few seconds, unsure of what she'd seen.

"Are you all right?" she asked. "You don't look good at all."

Chris breathed in deeply and exhaled through his teeth. "I don't know. I think I'm going to go lie down for a while. Are you going to be okay?"

Tori shrugged. "Yeah. I'll be fine. I'm probably going to rest a while myself."

She took up the task of cleaning the few dishes remaining in the sink as he padded down the hallway to his room and closed the door. The dirty window that looked out on the back yard over the faucet displayed smudges and ghostly strands of spiderwebs that cast a sinister pall over the unkempt yard. Through the knot of weeds, she spied locks of red-blonde hair. The cold sunshine spilled down upon it, and it sparkled like spun gold. A little girl dressed in a pair of burgundy pants and a long-sleeved, striped shirt sat on a swing, her back to the house. Tori dried her hands on a thin cotton towel, slipped her sneakers back on, and walked outside. The child rocked back and forth on the swing. Tori descended the steps to an overgrown pathway made up of flat rocks.

The wind died down and the air was static and stale. It no longer smelled like saltwater. It smelled like wet earth and the rot from dead leaves. The quiet unnerved her, but she trudged through the dew-dampened grass to the rusty playset. A pink plastic playhouse, sunbaked and moss-coated, had transformed over decades into a unique planter. Grasses and vines exploded from the open windows and doors.

The chains of the swing *screee-scraw*ed as the girl pushed herself back and forth. Tori felt awkward approaching her. She didn't want to alarm her, but she also didn't know if Chris would approve of someone playing on the set. She assumed it had once belonged to his daughter, and the thought made her stomach drop. Even so, the whole back yard looked like a tetanus shot waiting to happen.

"Excuse me," she said in a pitch much higher than her normal speaking voice. "Do you live around here? I don't know if Mr. Silver wants anyone out here. This set is very old, and you might get hurt."

The girl didn't acknowledge her and continued swinging back and forth, her back to Tori. Tori edged forward and extended a hand to touch the girl but thought better of it before she could make contact with her shoulder. Instead, she walked around the side of the set. A thorny stem raked across her leg, and a stinging pain slashed its way down her shin.

"Shit!" She put her hand over her mouth before she'd even gotten the expletive out.

She squeezed her way between the hedge and the back of the swing set and knelt in front of the girl.

"Honey, where do you live," she said, staring down at the girl's tiny, pink sneakers. "I'll walk you back ..."

Tori lifted her gaze and fell backward into the spiky hedge behind her. There was no face. Only a mass of hair. It ruffled like silk on the wind. Tori shrieked, the sound echoing off the trees, and slices of the child trailed off onto the breeze.

She reeled forward onto her hands and knees and pushed herself to her feet. A threatening presence hovered over her. It was inexplicable. The child was gone, but the sensation that an angry entity wanted her out pervaded the air.

The pressure of someone following her chased her back into the house. She looked over her shoulder to find nothing there, but she never stopped running until she was safely inside and slammed the door.

She darted to Chris's room and pounded on the door.

"Please, let me in," she hollered at the small crack between the door and the jamb.

Something shuffled around inside, and footfalls approached the door. A click followed, and Chris swung the door open. His face was drained of color. Tears collected at his lash line, and she stumbled inside.

"There's something outside," she sputtered. "A little girl, except she didn't have a face. There was only hair."

Her breath came in convulsive hitches. "When I tried to talk to her, she flittered away."

Chris's expression did not change. He looked down at the floor and brushed away the clot of tears at his eyes.

"It's my daughter," he told her, his voice measured and calm. "She visits me sometimes. Usually when things are hard."

Tori studied him carefully. His eyes were dark and puffed beneath. He looked weak and drawn.

"Listen, it's fine. It'll be okay. I need to lie down," he said, turning and leaving her shaken and terrified.

Chris walked back to his bed and flung himself onto it. Clothes were strewn about the floor, and his sheets were only halfway on the mattress. A corner of white quilting was exposed. She walked back out, more confused than ever.

It had to have been a hallucination. One of the pamphlets she'd read at Amelia's place said hallucinations weren't an uncommon withdrawal symptom. She pulled Chris's bedroom door shut on her way out, concerned about him and his behavior but determined not to bite the hand that had literally just fed her. She needed help now. No two ways about it. If she didn't get help, she was going to die.

Another wave of grief smacked Chris so hard, his shoulders heaved. More than twenty years he'd been sober. He'd had the urge from time to time, a longing to just have one drink. Each time, his resolve had been strong enough. The memory of his wife and girl was enough to pull him back from the brink. Something snaked through his guts and twisted so hard, he curled into the fetal position and rocked back and forth.

The voice started talking to him at the AA meeting. God, the things it said to him wrecked his head. It taunted him, volleyed invectives at him, used his baby against him. It spat visions of his daughter, lifeless and crumpled after the accident, into his head. The anxiety those words caused made his hands tremble. The back of his neck sweated, and his temples throbbed. If only he could take the edge off.

What difference does it make now? You're an old man. You've had a whole lifetime. It's more than your wife and kid got.

Did it matter now? Wouldn't just one drink take the edge off? He felt like he could claw his way through the mattress. Knowing that Emmy visited killed him inside. He rolled himself off of the mattress and hit the floor with his knees. They cracked, and he winced at the pain.

You should watch out for the bitch in your house. She's killed before. A kid, no less.

Chris struggled to his feet and walked to the window. He peeled the edge of the curtain back, unsure if he really wanted to see her there. Her face appeared on the other side of the curtain, nose pressed to the screen, eyes blackened and wide. Chris jerked the curtain shut again, unsure if he'd really seen her. He touched the curtain edge again, horrified to pull it back but unable to stop himself from doing so. It was irrational that she should be there. Even if she was real, there's no way a two-year-old could see into his window from the ground.

Are you rationalizing ghosts? What kind of dumb shit are you?

He pulled the edge of the curtain back again and caught sight of her hair. Her skin, smooth and plump, was pressed against the screen. Her button nose was flattened. She stared quizzically inside.

A pain it had taken him more than thirty years to bury ripped open inside him and he cried out. His face contorted, mouth agape, as a flood of tears erupted.

He tried to summon QuickSilver, but there was no response. He'd never tried to use it to save himself. He didn't even know if that was possible. Chris felt like a man who'd been abandoned in the desert. He had an oasis inside him, but he couldn't tap it. Something had taken up residence inside him and laid claim to it. His chest felt like a rubber band pulled taut in the throes of his panic as he tried again and again to access the hero within him.

You know what will help. Go on upstairs. It's waiting for you.

How could it have known? He'd forgotten about them himself., even in his most desperate moments. How many years had it been up there? At least a decade ago, he'd hit a low point. Emmy had been in the yard for days, tormenting him, tearing away at his already-frayed nerves. He'd walked down to the bait 'n tackle, mostly to clear his head. That's what he told himself anyway. The newsstand by the window kept him busy for a few minutes. He thumbed through the latest issue of *Flights of Fantasy*, paced up and down the aisles, and read the nutritional information label on every bag of chips on the rack. Eventually, he'd come to the beer cooler in the back. His whole body had trembled looking at the six packs. He decided on Old Milwaukee, the shittiest beer known to man. What if he only drank one? He could prove to himself that he had willpower if he could stop at one.

He'd opened the cooler and it chilled the sweat to his skin. The six pack felt heavier than any six pack he'd ever carried as he took it to the counter. Dave had smiled as he rang up the order, but Chris felt the judgment behind it. Guilt washed over him as he passed him a twenty and waited for his change.

The walk back home took twice as long as it should have as he'd wrestled with the beer and the even heavier choice of whether to drink it. By the time he got home, the decision had been made. He couldn't do this to himself. He couldn't desecrate the memory of his wife and child by poisoning himself.

The weight of that decision pressed on him even now. The voice that spoke to him gnawed at the back of his neck like a mosquito, buzzing and nagging until he felt hot and angry.

You remember where you left it, right? Of course you remember.

Chris wrung his hands and shuffled over the same worn patch of carpet again and again. His fingers tangled themselves in his hair. Just one wouldn't hurt.

He put a hand on the doorknob, walked into the hallway, and pulled down the ladder to the attic. He stepped gingerly up the rickety stairs into the stifling air of the darkened attic and batted around for the light string.

It smelled musty. Cardboard boxes were stacked one on top of the other. Cobwebs reflected the light. Something scampered around in the far reaches of the attic, some critter or another. A plastic Christmas tree stood undecorated in the corner.

Chris knelt at a box of waterlogged comic books, the salvaged remains of a flood he'd had back at the shop on Beach. Beneath the wrinkled, brown-stained paper he saw the six metal cylinders. They might as well have been bullets he could put in a revolver to blow his brains out. He ran a hand over the aluminum. They felt cold and smooth. Clinical. He pulled one of the cans from its plastic ring and studied it. It looked both alien and familiar at once. It had been a long, long time. He pulled the tab. It hissed.

www.ingramcontent.com/pod-product-compliance
Lightning Source LLC
Chambersburg PA
CBHW020611310726
48979CB00008B/1434/J

* 9 7 8 1 9 4 9 1 4 0 0 7 1 *